YA
MCCLEL   To Dance
TO

McClellan

D0868372

To Dance

Stephen McClellan

HURON PUBLIC LIBRARY
521 DAKOTA AVE S
HURON, SD 57350-2797

ISBN 978-1-64299-231-1 (paperback)
ISBN 978-1-64299-232-8 (digital)

Copyright © 2018 by Stephen McClellan

All rights reserved. No part of this publication may be reproduced, distributed, or transmitted in any form or by any means, including photocopying, recording, or other electronic or mechanical methods without the prior written permission of the publisher. For permission requests, solicit the publisher via the address below.

Christian Faith Publishing, Inc.
832 Park Avenue
Meadville, PA 16335
www.christianfaithpublishing.com

Printed in the United States of America

Dedication

To my wife Megan and the hope of tomorrow;
both the joys of my life

DISCARDED
HURON PUBLIC LIBRARY

Contents

Part2: The World of White

Part 1

Colorblind

August 18, 2016:
What to Do When the Clouds Grow Dark

A few days ago, I was walking home from school. The sun had left, the rain had come, and my Spider-Man backpack was getting soaked. But I danced in the puddles and sang to the sky because that's what you do when the clouds grow dark. I used to think that all people did that when the clouds got dark, but I am beginning to realize that some people see the sky a little different than other people.

Like when we went to *the* funeral. After I had thrown my rose in the grave and gone back to stand by Mother, the sky clapped. Through sniffles and tears, she had said, "Come on, Royce. We've seen enough rain for one day," which I considered the darndest thing because it had been sunny all day up until that point. It just hadn't made any sense. But back at the house, after Mother had disappeared under a blanket on the couch, Uncle Billy took my hand and led me outside.

I still remember trying to figure out what he had planned when *he* did the darndest thing. He held out his arms and tilted his face toward the sky, like he was expecting the Almighty himself to come down. He started smiling, which confused me even more, but then he said, "Royce, heaven mourns in its own way. When it does, it sends healing rain. Never miss an opportunity to let the rain wash you clean."

So we stood right there in the yard with our arms outstretched, Uncle Billy looking at the sky and me looking at Uncle Billy. Then, a raindrop fell, and we closed our eyes and prepared for the storm. That's how Mother had looked at the clouds, and that's how Uncle Billy had looked at the clouds. Both were looking at the same sky but had seen different things.

That was the day that my favorite habit was born: jumping into puddles. I love puddles! The darker the cloud means the bigger the rain, but the bigger the rain means the larger the puddle. I have made it a game of sorts, to find the largest puddle. Uncle Billy once told me that sometimes when you hunt deer, you let the smaller ones go because you are waiting on the bigger ones. "The ones worth putting on your wall," he says. That's how I have started viewing puddles. Let the smaller ones go, and hold out for the ones that matter. That's where the real splashes wait. Real splashes rise so high on either side of you that you feel like Moses walking through the walls of water.

The afternoon of the funeral was the first time that I have ever jumped into a puddle that meant something. Jumping into clean puddles is much different than jumping into dirty puddles. And I don't mean the color of the water. I mean the way it makes your heart feel. There was a lot to feel that day. I just wish Mother had jumped in the puddles with me. I think she needed some clean puddles to splash through.

And I sing. Oh, how I sing! Most of the time it is the tune from the TV show that Grandpa Don used to watch before the cancer got the best of him. "*. . . the moo-vie star. Ginger and Marie Anne. Here on Gilliland's isleeeee!*" Sometimes it rains so hard that I imagine that the whole earth is swallowed up with water except the patch of cracked sidewalk that I am skipping down. It becomes my own personal island. That's why I always think of that song. Some songs just fit the moment and deserve to be sung. It's a shame not give them their due.

Although I like to dance in the puddles and sing to the sky, I know that people have other ways of celebrating the dark clouds. Across the street, John Mark always takes one of his toy rowboats and sends it merrily down the stream. He said that he never chases it, just watches the water bob it from side to side as it floats away. Mrs.

Cloggins, from 4B, takes all seven of her flowerpots out from under the protection of her balcony canopy. "Cotton Top" Cody (kids at school call him that because of his white hair) reads a comic book while lying on his stomach on his porch. "Old Man" Riggins, my neighbor on the left, strums his guitar to old tunes that only my Grandpa Don would have been able to recognize. (Riggins always hums the words more than sings them, like most elderly folks do.)

My mother is different. She always curses the dark clouds because they remind her of how good days can turn bad. Like the day that she looked through a windshield at rain pattering down. While she waited for the light to turn from red to green, the wipers swatted at the rain like you would swat at an annoying fly. (That's the detail that she always seems to remember the best, although she rarely talks about it.) That was *the* day, the last day that I saw her genuinely smile. Actually, she has smiled since then, but smiles don't matter much unless they are genuine. That's what I have always thought.

It was raining earlier today. The puddles were exceptionally big, so I sang exceptionally loud. I saw a car approaching and hurried over to the sidewalk. I held out my arms and tilted my face to the sky, like my uncle showed me how to do years ago. The car rushed through the puddle next to the street, sending a tidal wave over my body. I smiled and let the water do its thing. Never miss an opportunity to let the rain wash you clean.

There are a lot of things to do when the clouds get dark, but there are only two that fit my liking: I sing loud, and I jump high. If you sing loud enough and jump high enough, then maybe the water can make your world disappear. Maybe all people need is to see the world through a wall of water.

Most people know that life can be a storm. The darker the clouds get, the harder it rains. But the way I see it, the harder it rains, the cleaner you get! You just have to learn to dance in the rain first. I am learning to do that, I think.

August 29, 2016:
Walks Home

I had to walk home from school again today because Mother forgot to pick me up. I have been in school for three weeks, so you would think that she could have gotten used to the routine by now. I'm not in her mind though, and I don't know what she is thinking, so I guess I shouldn't speak ill of her. Really, it didn't upset me that much. I love being outside and feeling the sunshine on my face. Since it was a sunny day, it was a good day to be forgotten.

I love breathing in fresh air. It makes me feel alive. In class, Ms. Sempsrott said that we need air to live, but Uncle Billy once said that we need hope to live. I'm still not sure which one it is. If Uncle Billy is right, then we wouldn't need to breathe in air, we would need to breathe in hope. What if it was backwards and air was really called hope?

Then, it would be hope that fills our lungs.

That makes me wonder what life would be like if a lot of things were backwards. Like, what if elbows were really called bellybuttons, or toes really called ears? I remember Pastor Scoggins telling us at Vacation Bible School a few years ago that if we wanted to be first then we needed to be last. It seemed strange to me, but I decided to try it out and got last in line at snack time. I thought that the gesture would earn me three gold stickers on heaven's whiteboard. But guess what happened? I stayed last in line, and no one ever put me in the front, and all the good snacks were taken by the time it was my turn. Life can be confusing all right.

What I love the most about my walks home is that I get to see all sorts of interesting things. Some people hate walking home, but I think it's because they haven't learned how to see yet. The world really is waiting to tell you things if you just quit arguing long enough to listen.

There are always people to watch, and I have learned them well. I even have nicknames for them all. Like "Nike Man" for example. He is always running with headphones on and dressed completely in Nike gear—headband, shirt, shorts, socks, and shoes. He pumps his fists like he just won a race and mouths the words to whatever song he is listening to. I always try to watch his lips and guess what song is playing.

Then, there is "Sweet Tooth Nana." She isn't actually my nana, but she is old just like my nana and looks kind of like her too. She is always sitting outside on her patio eating ice cream when I walk by. From the color of it, it looks to be cotton candy, but I am not sure. She always waves to me, and I wave back, because that's the polite thing to do when people acknowledge you.

"Ma'am Talk-A-Lot," with the sunglasses, always paces down the sidewalk impatiently, as if the sidewalk has insulted her casserole or something. She carries a hand weight in one hand and her cell phone in the other. When she talks, she throws her head back and waves the hand weight around in frustration.

The "Man in Grey" always walks a pit bull that looks like it weighs more than he does. The "Hydrant Gang" is a group of kids who are a little younger than me who always play on a patch of grass near the fire hydrant. The "Rainbow Man" is an old man who always sits on the corner of Tifton Street and paints pictures of everything he sees. His coat is always stained with different colors, which makes me think about how many paintings those colors have made over the years.

If I'm honest, who I really like to watch are the ones that look like they have a story to tell. They never follow the same routine, and you usually only see them once. They are always a mystery. Like one time, I saw a woman crying on a park bench while holding a jacket. I imagined that the jacket represented a sad memory. Maybe she found out that someone had died, or that she had gotten fired, or that her favorite pet had run away, or that her boyfriend was angry . . . or maybe, they were even tears of joy! I hadn't walked in her shoes, so I couldn't say how they fit. Uncle Billy told me that it is best to not judge people if I hadn't walked in their shoes.

Another time, I saw a man walking down the middle of the street smiling and singing. Not even the side of the street. The middle! What had made him so happy? Was he happy because he had a family, or because he was wearing his lucky shoes, or because he won the lottery? Maybe he was happy because he had no reason to be sad? Then, there was the boy riding a skateboard that had long hair and a tattoo of a snake wrapped around his arm. Why was it there? What did it mean? Did he get the tattoo because he loved snakes or because he was afraid of snakes? To me, the things that make us afraid are much more important to us than the things that make us happy. Not because we like them more, but because we seem to pay more attention to the things that make us afraid. In that case, maybe the boy got the tattoo to remind himself that he doesn't need to focus on the things that make him scared.

There are always people to watch, and I never get tired of looking. If you have a big imagination, then there is always a story to tell (even when people don't want to tell their own story). I just do that part for them, and usually the story comes out fairly nice. Sometimes I wish I could tell people how wonderful their story is in my mind. Then, maybe they would choose to change the story that they have and make a better one—one that makes them genuinely smile.

We never know what someone's story is. The person walking down the street that we pay no attention to and forget quickly because we are late for that practice, or that class, or that meeting, or that homework assignment. I wish that I could actually put on their shoes for the day and become them, or be the video camera that sees through their eyes. Then, I would know why people laugh, or cry, or sing, or paint, or get snake tattoos. I would understand why the world is the way it is and why people fill it the way they do. I have tried harder to see the world differently and see what other people choose not to see. Life is more interesting that way.

I read a story in a book today at school, and even though I am still trying to figure it out completely, it seems like it relates to what I'm trying to say. I copied it word for word so that I wouldn't mess it up. I hope it helps you on your next walk home.

"There is More"
By Master Cho-Tri Zen

A student approached his master who was meditating peacefully. "Master," he said, "Teach me about life—how to love, how to appreciate, and how to pursue."

The master thought for a moment and then responded, "Follow me."

The elder walked outside with the younger close behind him. Neither of them spoke. Soon, they had reached the forest where large trees formed a canopy above them. The master said, "Look around you. What do you think?"

The student turned in a circle, viewing his surroundings. "I think that we are in a forest surrounded by a lot of trees . . . trees that are good for climbing."

"Indeed we are," said the master, "but have you considered how the trees grew to be the size they are now? Their colors, their leaves, their height, their shape, or the vast expanse of nature in which they find life?"

"I have not," replied the student.

The master spoke, "We must do more than think. We must reflect."

The master and the student wove their way through the forest until they approached a large waterfall. The master said, "Look at the water. What do you see?"

The student paused, narrowed his gaze, and replied, "I see a fresh source of running water and a waterfall that would be fun to play in."

The master took the student by the shoulders and pointed to the heart of the waterfall. "Look closer," he said. The student focused his gaze in the direction the master was pointing. A beam of sunlight had broken through the trees. Where it intersected with the falling water, a beautiful array of colors shone in the mist.

"You see," said the master, "We must do more than look. We must observe."

The master led the student away from the waterfall. As they strolled along the path, the master stopped and knelt to the ground. He picked up a flower and handed it to the student. "Touch this flower. What do you recognize?"

The student held the flower, somewhat perplexed. "This flower is pretty, but it is weak. It will die soon."

The master took the flower from the student and softly massaged its petals. "This flower is still coated with tiny droplets of morning dew, signifying that it has lived to see another day. The petals are like smooth skin without any defects."

"So what does that mean?" asked the student.

The master replied, "We must do more than touch. We must feel."

As the two continued their journey side by side, the forest woke to new life. The master asked the student, "What do you hear?"

The student paused for a moment and turned his ear toward the sky. "I hear the chirping of birds echoing in the treetops."

"You are correct," said the master. "However, pay even closer attention to the chirping you hear."

The student remained completely still and closed his eyes to concentrate. He began to recognize the individual rhythms of each sound as every bird sang its own unique melody to each other. The student smiled. "It sounds beautiful."

The master nodded in approval and said, "We must do more than hear. We must listen."

Soon, they returned to the small cottage from which they had first embarked. A butterfly landed on the edge of the roof and sat motionless. The master turned to the student and asked, "What do you think about the existence of this butterfly?"

The student pondered while the master waited patiently. Finally, he spoke. "I think that the butterfly is a pleasant creature who causes no harm."

"That is a good observation," answered the master. "Although to understand the existence of the butterfly, you must not look at its life, but at its death. Butterflies only live a few weeks, and in some cases, only a few days. They do not waste their time on needless pleasures, but rather, seek to find true love and reproduce life. Every day of their life serves a purpose." The butterfly slowly spread its wings. Hues of blue and orange shimmered under the rays of sunlight.

"You see," said the master, "We must do more than exist. We must live."

The student stopped at the base of the steps that led into the cottage. "Master, I have seen what you have revealed to me, and I am beginning to understand how to apply these areas in my pursuit of an abundant life. But I still have one more question. What is the root of it all?"

The master looked pleased. "That, my young learner, is the most important question of all. The answer, to which, you already possess within yourself."

"How do I possess it?" asked the student.

The master replied, "Everyone has a brain, but not everyone chooses to reflect. Everyone has eyes, but not everyone chooses to observe. Everyone has fingers, but not everyone chooses to feel. Everyone has ears, but not everyone chooses to listen. Everyone has life, but not everyone chooses to live. Everyone can learn, but not everyone chooses to apply that learning. Therein, lies your answer."

The master mounted the steps and opened the door. The student called after him, "I do not understand. Where do I begin?"

The master turned to face his student and smiled. "You choose."

September 15, 2016: Masks

My teacher is an interesting lady. She is always reading *People Magazine* when we walk into class every morning. Occasionally, she will scoff at something and roll her eyes, take a sip of tea, push her glasses back up her nose, and turn the page. When she looks up at us, we quickly look away. We know better than to bother her during her morning time of catching-up-on-the-world's-gossip.

Come to think of it, Ms. Sempsrott has several daily routines. She wears the same sweater every day, although she has on a different shirt under it. (Well, usually she does, but not every time.) She reads the same magazine every day and drinks the same tea every day. It's Country Peach Passion tea. She even starts off the day with the same greeting: "Good morning my young learners! Are we ready?" I say yes because sometimes it's wise to tell people what they want to hear. Although, most of the time I am actually *not* ready to start another day of school work.

She also wears the same necklace every day. It's a locket that she tries to hide, but sometimes it shows when she bends down to pick something off the floor. Casey Deal claims that she came in early from recess one day and saw Ms. Sempsrott looking at a picture in the locket, but no one believes her much. Ms. Sempsrott is very secretive about it.

Today, we were learning how to come up with rhyming words. She gave us an assignment to write a poem, but we could only use the word that she assigned us individually. When I unfolded the piece of paper that she had placed on my desk, I saw the word *brown*. I knew a Mr. Brown that lived down the street from me a few years ago, so I decided to write about him. I sat thinking for a few minutes, then wrote:

> Why, oh why, cried Mr. Brown, Must I wear the
> face of a clown?
> This old town is bringing me down!
> Why must I be a clown in this town?
> The mask wears a smile, but I wear a frown.
> Why, oh why, cried Mr. Brown.

I thought it was good, but Ms. Sempsrott did not seem very impressed. Actually, I don't even think she read it all. She swallowed hard, set the paper down lightly, and turned around to clear her throat. It was like it was hard for her to read or something. But then, when she turned back around, she seemed fine. I think she was wearing a mask herself in that moment. It was a discouraged mask, a lonely mask, a heavy mask.

I wanted to help her, but I couldn't. It wasn't my mask to wear.

Maybe there is a picture in that locket, and maybe that picture makes Ms. Sempsrott sad. If so, she has to make a happy mask. Those are the easiest kind to make because smiles make people think that everything is all right. We can never tell what kind of masks people have in their closets, or how many. I have a feeling that Ms. Sempsrott's closet of masks is very long. Very long indeed.

September 22, 2016:
Mother

Mother gave me the opportunity to walk home from school again today. It *has* started to worry me a little bit when she forgets to pick me up, but I try not to let it bother me more than it should.

I know that Mother is still "getting back on her feet." That's the way that Uncle Billy puts it. But I will say that two years is a long time to try and stand up again. When I was a baby, Mother said that it only took me eight months to stand on my own. I know it's not exactly the same thing, but it still seems like she should be getting the strength back in her legs.

When I am trying to understand adults, I always try to relate it to school in some way. Last year, a bully shoved me down in the sand on the playground. I kept trying to stand up, but the bully kept pushing me down. Finally, a teacher saw what was happening and ran over to make him stop.

I think maybe Mother's condition is something like that. Maybe a bully has beaten her up, and every time that she tries to stand back up, the bully pushes her down again. But who is the bully? I don't think that I have seen anyone pushing her. She used to talk about how Uncle Billy and her would wrestle on the ground when they were younger, but he hasn't been around lately, so it couldn't be him. Plus, he isn't the bullying type.

If Uncle Billy isn't the bully, then who is? Maybe it's someone that I can't see. I heard my mother yelling at Uncle Billy days after the funeral. I have never forgotten what she said because I thought it was really strange. She said, "He is just sitting up there watching all of this happen, and we have to be the ones to pick up the broken pieces!"

I have always wondered who "he" is and what "up there" means. I'm sure one day I will find out, when someone is ready to tell me.

I have noticed a few changes in Mother. She works down at the local Roses retail store as a cashier. I love Roses because they have really good toys. Every time a new shipment of toys comes in, I always get the first look at things since Mother works there. She hasn't brought me home a gift since the funeral though. This makes me sad. Not because I am obsessed with toys, but because toys mean that Mother isn't sad. No toys mean that she is hurting, and I don't like to see her hurting. I think that she has a mask of her own. It's the sadness mask. I think she has gotten rid of all the other masks in her closet except for that one.

She never tells me that she is hurting, or how badly. She just complains of being tired and drinks out of a brown paper bag more often. She says it is a special wrapper with special powers. It must be really powerful because she wears it around every drink that she has in her hand.

She also sleeps a little more. Well, a lot more. She is always sleeping when I walk in from school. Sometimes, she looks so peaceful sleeping that it puts *me* at peace. It takes my worries away. Ms. Sempsrott says that your body needs rest in order to have energy and that the more energy you use, the better you will sleep. Mother doesn't seem to follow that cycle. She can sleep as much as she wants. Even when she is awake, her eyes look like they are tired. Bless her heart.

The last thing I have noticed is that Mother reads a lot. I once told her that if she loved reading so much, I could bring her a few books from our library at school. She didn't want that. Apparently, she is very particular about the books that she reads. Her favorite book has a brown leather cover with no name or title on it. She uses a picture of my dad as a bookmark for it. Sometimes, she will sit on the couch for hours and read through it. She usually cries, which I think is strange because I have never cried when reading one of my books. I was sad when Old Yeller died, but I still didn't cry. It's just a book, and it's not real. That's what I always say to remind myself to stay happy. Maybe Mother doesn't know that it's not real. If she only knew that a book couldn't hurt her, then everything would be all right!

My mother is a good mother though. She is kind and loving and lets me stay up as long as I want. Not even Jimmy Smolgy's mother allows him to do that, and she has a reputation of being the coolest mother in school! It makes me proud of my own mother.

She tries hard, and that's all that matters. I know that I can't take her sadness away, but I *can* help bring a little more happiness into her life. We all deserve that much.

October 10, 2016:
The Field

There are good walks home, and there are bad walks home. I wish I could say they are all good, but that just isn't so. The thing is, there must be some bad mixed in with the good, or else the good wouldn't fit right. Sometimes, the bad reminds me of how good the good really is. So I guess I'll take the bad once in a while.

The walk home today started off beautiful. Everything was *very*—the grass was *very* green, the wind was *very* soothing, the skies were *very* blue, and the clouds were *very* white. I thought the clouds looked about as white as our back field looks after a fresh fallen snow (before the neighborhood kids romp through it and leave pudgy tracks). It made me want to rush down the clouds on my sled with my hands in the air and my earmuffs pulled tightly around my head.

On most occasions, I follow Hideaway Street until it dead ends, and then I turn onto Country Way for the remainder of the walk. That route home takes a bit longer, but you see a lot more interesting people than you do otherwise. But I didn't have time for that today. Today was special. A new season of *Power Rangers* was starting, and I was itching to see the first episode. Last season left off with Zordon creating a new ranger, but the episode ended before they revealed who it was. I have just about gone crazy the last couple of months waiting to find out.

I decided to take a shortcut through Morganton Point. There are two baseball fields at the Point: the upper field and the lower field.

HURON PUBLIC LIBRARY
521 DAKOTA AVE S
HURON, SD 57350-2797

The upper field is a nice field that different schools in the county like to use. The lower field is deserted and has a short patch of woods that lies beyond the crusted outfield fence. That trail dumps out right around the corner from my apartment. It is a lonely walk that I never make at nighttime. I have heard too many tall tales from the locals to trust going that way past sundown.

A team was practicing on the upper field, so I walked around the dugouts and hopped the fence that led to the lower field. I picked up a piece of grass and was chewing on it casually, whistling as I went. All I could think about was the green ranger, and Zordon, and who the new ranger could be. And okay, I admit I was thinking about the pink ranger as well because she is really, really pretty. Things were normal, as most days are when something gets in the way.

As I started walking through right field toward the patch of woods, a muffled racket caught my attention. I looked across the field to where home plate used to be. In the shadows, a big kid was punching a small kid, and the small kid was crying. I didn't recognize either one, which meant I couldn't make heads from tails. It was obvious that the fight wasn't fair, but what could I do? I tried to think of something quickly, but my mind wouldn't cooperate. All I could do was stand there frozen in place, staring at the two boys.

The big kid threw one last punch, causing the small boy to collapse to the ground. The boy's face was hidden in the dirt with his hands protecting his head. The big kid shook his fist at the boy and started saying something. The wind was blowing a hair too loud for me to hear everything he said, but I caught the last few words . . . "You must be colorblind or something. You're nothing but a nig-ger—she's not. Don't let me catch you talking to her again. You just stick to your people and we'll stick to ours."

The boy on the ground looked over and caught me staring. The whites of his eyes loomed so big that they seemed to swallow me whole. In that moment, I felt like I knew real fear. The big kid swung around to see what he was looking at, and once he did, my mind didn't need any more motivation. I started sprinting toward the outfield fence, too scared to look behind me.

I have heard the word *nigger* only one time before in my life. That was from Joey Stokes, who claimed that he had heard it from a movie that his old man had been watching. Joey had thought it was funny, while this big kid didn't seem to think it was funny at all. I don't know exactly what the word means, but in either case, I don't care to find out. Anything negative isn't worth finding out anyway. Mother is calling for dinner. I'll try to be quick . . .

October 10, 2016:
Why We Run

S orry about that. Mother hates it for the food to get cold, so I didn't want to upset her. She had just gotten up from a long nap, and she said her head hurt. I figured it was best to not make things harder for her. I have just a few more thoughts about the day before I let you go. I'll try not to make it long.

Picking up my story from today . . . I ran until my side hurt, and my head hurt even more. It was the type of running where you can feel your face pulsing, like it's going to explode ten shades of red. Soon, I popped out of the trees and was back on the road. I whizzed past Mr. Falkirk's bakery and past the construction site of the new grocery store. I think it's amazing how far I can run when fear is pushing me. Fear and I need to buddy up on the playground the next time we play tag at school.

By the time I got home, my shirt was so drenched with sweat that you could have wrung it out. I leaned against the bricks of our apartment complex, panting and dry mouthed. I turned around, half expecting to see the big boy chasing me. But like all great fantasies, there was nothing to see but trees slow dancing with the wind. I let out a huge sigh and sat down on the ground. There was no need to rush inside at that point. It got me thinking about why we run. People are always running from things but for different reasons. Miss Jane, my neighbor to the right, once told Mother that she was constantly moving around and hadn't seen her family in twelve years. When Miss Jane walked away, Mother turned to me and said, "She's running from something." It made me think that maybe what we run *from* is much more important than what we run *to*.

A couple years ago, I wanted Mother to play tag with me, but she said, "I don't run unless someone is chasing me!" That seemed like a good enough reason for me (even though I tried to chase her, but she kept reading the paper and paid no attention).

Last fall, Uncle Billy came to watch one of my football games. When I intercepted a pass, I could hear him yelling from the sideline, "Run like hell's chasing you, Royce!" My classmates run in PE while playing games, and the "Hydrant Gang" ran out of the haunted house down by the mill last Halloween, screaming their heads off.

One day, "Old Man" Riggins stopped playing his guitar long enough to have a chat with me. He told me that he hadn't talked to his son in nearly three years. I told him it was about time to make that call wasn't it, but he just said that he had been on the run for too long, and when you have been running that long, that's all you know how to do. I guess the bad kind of running can become a habit. Seems like it would be easier not to form the habit in the first place, but maybe grownups know something that I don't.

I once gave a Valentine's Day card to a girl in my class. Scarlet was her name. It had an image of Aladdin handing a chocolate heart to Jasmine. It read, "Will you be my Princess?" She started blushing and ran right out of the classroom and into the girl's bathroom. I felt bad at first, but after lunch, I found a note in my cubbyhole with one word written on it: "Yes." That's when I knew that not all running was bad. We just have to choose to run at the right time.

It's funny, the things we run from. Sometimes, we don't even know *what* we are running from. All we know is that we need to run faster, or longer, or harder; that if we outrun it, then we won't have to face it. But that's the farthest thing from the truth! Life finds us, and sometimes we just have to stand up to it. If we don't, life will just keep chasing us until we decide to do something about it. I am going to try and stop running from the wrong things in my life.

I think that's all for tonight. It's been a long day, and I need some rest.

October 25, 2016:
How to Pray

I walked inside today and said hi to Mother, but she couldn't hear me because she was asleep on the couch with a bottle tucked under her arm. I turned off the TV, pulled a blanket from the closet, and draped it over her. She had probably had a rough day. Maybe not physically rough, but still. I ran upstairs to my room and shut the door behind me. I needed some time to think. It's been two weeks, and the images of the field have clung to me the way peanut butter clings to the roof of my mouth. I can't get what happened out of my mind.

Why was the big kid so angry? Why did he have to take his anger out like that? I know you can't always trust what you see, but the small kid didn't look like he was someone who would do any harm (especially to someone that much bigger than himself). Every time I have shut my eyes, the whites of the boy's eyes have reached out for me. That day, they were terrified, and desperate, and helpless. And I had run away! I felt ashamed of it.

The big kid said that the small kid was colorblind. Did that mean that he couldn't see colors? There is a boy in the third grade at my school who gets his reds and greens mixed up. Although, the big kid was white, and the small kid was black, so I guess it's not exactly the same situation. It's still dealing with colors though, right? Why would the big kid care if the boy could see colors or not? The grass is green, the sky is blue, and people are people. No need to get all in a fuss over someone who can't see as good as you can.

There are so many things that I can't figure out. It's all too confusing. But, there *are* two things that I know for sure: 1. I want to love everyone, no matter how old they are, or how small, or how scared, and 2. I don't want to run anymore. Those are the only two things that seem to matter at the moment.

I didn't know where to begin, but I felt like I had to do something. I had already missed one opportunity to help the small kid, and I wasn't going to miss another. Pastor Scoggins always said that when you need help, but you don't know what to do, you should just pray.

"Two words, my brothers," he always claims while pounding the podium, "Just pray!" Then the deacons yell "Amen!" and "Preach it brother!"

I have been praying since I was a kid. Back then, it was all about the rhymes and songs. ("God is great, God is good, let us thank him for our food. By His hands we are fed, give us Lord our daily bread.") Of course, there was one time that I was eating dinner at Pastor Scoggins house because I am friends with his boy, Cody ("Cotton Top"). Pastor Scoggins asked Cody to bless the food, and Cody said, "Beans, beans, they're good for your heart. The more you eat em', the more you fart. The more you fart, the better you feel. Eat those beans for every meal!" Cody laughed so hard that his laugh turned silent. Not a sound came out of him, but his shoulders heaved, and tears ran down his cheeks. He was still wiping his tears when the pastor sent him to his room. That was a prayer I'll never forget. I don't figure God will forget it either. I bet he was getting a good laugh himself at that one. Imagining God laughing at something we do makes me smile every time.

Mother never prays anymore because she said that she has said too many prayers. I don't know if God has a limit or not, but if so, then that wouldn't make much sense. He is supposed to be the most powerful thing ever. Maybe Mother has run out of things to say, or maybe God sees the mess in the living room, or the smoky ashtray, or the brown bottle wrappings, and knows what she wants even without her asking. I like to think that God works that way.

Usually, I try to be grateful in my prayers, but sometimes I can't help but keep asking for stuff. Those times, I feel guilty because I feel like I'm asking God to keep giving me things when I haven't really given anything back. Sometimes, I can't think of what to say, so I'll just say "Hi," or "Thank you." I don't think there is anything wrong with those types of prayers because they are the genuine kind. And I think that God loves genuine things.

I decided that it was a good time for a prayer. I walked over to the window where I could get a good look at the sky. I have always felt more comfortable when I can see the sky. It makes me think that I can see God himself. It was a beautiful day. The clouds were putting on a show as if they were on Broadway. Animals, people, and ships all danced gracefully across the blue stage.

I knelt down and linked my fingers together because that's what Pastor Scoggins always does. I shouldn't know this because you are supposed to keep your eyes closed during the prayer, but I cheat sometimes to see what everyone else is doing. I have found that many of the kids have the same curiosity that I do.

I sat there for a minute thinking. The boy's face from the field once again floated in front of me. *Colorblind.* If the small boy was colorblind, then that's what I wanted to be as well. Even though I didn't fully understand it, I knew that anything was better than what the big kid stood for. I didn't know what to say, or how to say it, but I figured God knew those things. When I don't know how to start a writing assignment in school, Ms. Sempsrott always tells us, "Keep it simple!" So that's what I did. I closed my eyes, bowed my head, and prayed. "I pray I may, I pray I might, become colorblind and be given new sight."

October 26, 2016:
Things Change When You Pray

As soon as I walked into school this morning, I knew that my prayer last night had changed things. Every person looked different, yet similar in a way that I couldn't describe. They had different height, and clothes, and hair, but they all seemed to glow the same color. I thought that maybe I was still sleeping, but something told me that it was real. Most boys would have been scared, but I didn't worry. That's what happens when you pray. Things change.

I know this, in part, because of the stories that I have heard. There are some amazing ones! A few weeks back, Mrs. Mabel, who plays the piano at church and throws her head back when she sings, shared that she had been diagnosed with cancer. The church offered to pray for her, and everyone laid hands on her. She told the congregation the following week that the doctor's report had come back clean. *Spotless* was the word she used.

Johnny Lewis, or "Mr. Johnny" I should say to keep my manners, survived a car crash last spring. His mother claimed that a strange notion had come over her, so she immediately got on her knees and started praying. That ended up being the same time that Johnny was in the accident.

One time at school, Ms. Sempsrott got so annoyed with us that she rubbed her temples and said, "Lord Jesus, give me patience." Wouldn't you know it, the class got quiet, and she smiled and went on teaching.

Those are the good answers, the ones that make people smile and say things like, "Lord's protection," and "He watches over his people." Then, there are other prayers, the ones that are answered but not in the way people expect. These are especially confusing, and I don't know what to think about them. Like my friend Jaime who prayed for a toy train set last Christmas. He got the train set, but it wasn't the one that he wanted (or at least not the one that he had pictured in his mind). His prayer was answered and not answered at the same time.

Last year, our city was happy because the mayor that they wanted to get elected won all of the votes. Prayers answered. But then, he got caught up in some bad stuff and became corrupt and everything changed. Prayers not answered. Are prayers still considered answered even if people's minds change after the fact? I don't understand this. I think some people think they know what's good for them, but they don't really know, so then they aren't happy with the results of the answered prayers. They don't realize what they are praying for when they pray for it.

There are other prayers too, the ones that don't get answered. (Actually, I think they do, but sometimes God's answer is no, so they look like they haven't been answered at all). The plane crashes, or the heart attack happens, or the earthquake destroys, or the breaks go out entering the turn. These situations don't make any sense, and I have never really tried to make sense of them for that reason. The world is full of bad things, and lucky enough for me, I'm just a kid, so I'm not supposed to understand it all. Pastor Scoggins says that we aren't called to understand, but we *are* called to believe. "Faith of a mustard seed," he says.

So that's what I try to do. I keep praying, and I keep believing. What doesn't make sense to me are the people that quit praying all together. There isn't a lick of hope in not praying at all! I mean, I wouldn't just quit playing baseball if I lost one game. I would keep working. All that batting practice will pay off at some point I would think!

There are a lot of things that I don't know, but there is one thing that I do know: prayer changes things. And whether we like the change or not is really up to us. Either way, we have to live with the results. So I wasn't worried when things seemed different at school. Good or bad, that's exactly what I had prayed for.

November 3, 2016:
Sadness

I walked into the house after school and smelled a strange smell. One that I had smelled before. It made me think of my Uncle Billy. A long time ago, or so it seems, Uncle Billy slept over at our house for a few nights. (This was right before he "got his head on straight," as Mother put it.) The second night he was with us, he came in really late. I ran down the stairs to see him, but he was already snoring on the couch. When I walked into the living room the next morning, Uncle Billy was already gone. Mother was scrubbing the carpet. I didn't know what had happened, but the room smelled rotten. All Mother said was, "It's what happens when you drink too much, Royce."

Since then, I have always considered, "what happens when you drink too much" a scent in a long line of bad colognes. It could go in a collection with, "that's been sitting out too long," and "darn sewage system," and "those just need to be thrown out." Come to think of it, a lot of my mother's comments could be made into bad colognes.

I cupped my hands under the kitchen faucet and drank long and good. Then, I walked upstairs and found Mother sleeping on her bed with only one sock on. She had a picture of my father tucked under her arm. The smell was worse in her room. Much worse than Uncle Billy's had been.

I decided to surprise her and make her some soup. I snuck out of the room quietly (even though I didn't think a cement truck could have woken her) and walked down to the kitchen. I opened the refrigerator to see what we had to eat. I like our refrigerator because there aren't too many options. It makes picking easy. When we go to restaurants on rare occasions, there are too many things to choose from on the menu. It makes my brain hurt.

But our fridge isn't annoying like that. You get choice A, B, or C.

I looked at the yogurt and milk on the top shelf, the Lunchables on the middle shelf, and the Campbell's soup on the bottom shelf. I picked a can of Beef Potato and placed it in the microwave. All we had in the side door was Coke, so I poured some into a red Dixie cup. Once the microwave beeped, I took the soup and Coke up to Mother.

I had to shake her lightly to get her eyes to flitter open. She glanced down at the food and gave me a weak smile. She leaned forward and kissed me on the forehead. I told her that I needed to get some homework done, stood up, and skipped away. I came into my room, but instead of opening up my backpack, I got out my journal.

I don't really have homework, but I don't want to see my mother sad. I know that's why she is in bed. She always tries to hide it from me, but I know it is there. Sometimes, it's not in her words, but in the rings under her eyes, or the shaking in her hands, or in her strewn lipstick, or in her messy hair. It comes in different forms but always with the same message.

Mrs. Dorene, from 2C, shows her sadness by watching black and white romance movies and hugging a pillow. The homeless man down the road by the green bench shows his sadness by singing the blues. Jayden, a girl in my class, shows her sadness by drooping her hair in front of her face to hide while she cries. Mr. Perkins, our mailman, shows his sadness by smiling really big and wishing us a happy day.

It's interesting to watch the different ways that people show sadness. Some try to hide it and some don't, but sadness is like a dark cloud that covers people. No matter where they go or what they try to do, they can't make the cloud disappear. Everyone can see it. Those are the people that I think should learn how to dance the most when the clouds grow dark. After all, dancing is the only way to make the clouds go away.

November 8, 2016:
A Boy Named Kim

Sometimes, life happens when we least suspect it. I wasn't expecting what life threw at me today, but it happened all the same. I was walking down the hallway when I saw a boy spill his books on the ground. He looked a little helpless, and everyone was ignoring him, so I ran over to see if I could help. At first, he looked at me with a strange, almost suspicious look, but then he smiled and said thank you.

I had never seen him before, but he glowed the same unique color like everyone else. I asked where he was from, and he said that he was from a country very far away. It was pretty interesting actually. In his country, the streets are always crowded, and there is a lot of rich tradition. He said that people write in symbols instead of words and eat a lot of rice. I think I remember learning something about a big wall in history class last year, but I didn't want to embarrass myself by asking.

His family had just moved to the neighborhood. I asked him if he had made any friends yet. He hadn't. I said, "Well it's your lucky day because you just made your first friend. I'm Royce."

This put a smile on the boy's face, and he bowed as a gesture of thanks. He shook my hand and told me that his name was Kim. It reminded me of a girl's name, but I didn't say that to him of course. Kim is really cool, and I am lucky that he accidentally dropped his books when I was walking by.

It hadn't been a bad day at all. I got an A on my AR reading quiz, and I had made a new friend. But sometimes the devil knows when our day is looking ripe and decides to put his two cents into it. When I was walking back from the library, three big kids pushed me up against a locker. I cried out in surprise, but they looked angry, so I kept my mouth shut. They said every swear word I had heard of (plus some I hadn't heard of) and asked me why I had talked to the boy. They said that his people aren't like us and are no good for our country. They said that his people take our jobs and put our country in debt. Plus, they said, he has slanted eyes and looks strange.

I looked at the boys in front of me and thought that they had the same glow as Kim, but I didn't say anything. Sometimes it's wiser to keep your opinions to yourself. They said that they wanted my lunch. I didn't have a lot anyway, so I let them have it. One small Lunchable pack isn't worth getting beaten up over (even if it *is* Pepperoni, which is my favorite). After all, the boys aren't the ones who won the fight. I wish Uncle Billy could have seen how brave I was in that moment. I'll have to remember to tell him about it.

Some other kids saw the boys take off with my lunch, but they passed by on the other side of the hallway and didn't say a word. Maybe they were scared, or maybe they saw what I saw—that some people pick on other people because something is missing in their lives. I pity those people. But on the positive side, I have a new friend named Kim, and I am mighty proud of him.

November 9, 2016:
To Be Popular

I woke up early with a lot on my mind, so I think I'll write a few thoughts before leaving for school. What the boys did yesterday has really bothered me. They probably just wanted to fit in, I think. Isn't that what everyone really wants? To know that they belong? To know that they are important? To know that people like them? I think it's worse in school. In school, kids face issues that even some grownups don't face. Well, I guess those grownups might have faced them when they were kids, but times change, so I don't know if you can really compare it or not. There is so much pressure that it's suffocating. It convinces girls to wear too much lip gloss, boys to wear too much Axe body spray, and teachers to try and piece it all together.

It's amazing what some people will do to get attention. One time, Watson Baggat told me a story about his older brother Henry. Henry went to a party a few months back. Henry is in high school, so he is allowed to do that. Well, it was a party with a lot of older kids and a lot of pretty girls (two things that make us young boys nervous). He decided to make a name for himself, so he took off all his clothes and used his cowboy hat to hide his private part. Then, he ran out from behind the bushes and jumped off the diving board into the pool, bare butt and all. Apparently, everyone loved it and started laughing! His nickname has been "The Outlaw" ever since. Watson laughed as he told the story, but all I could think about was how dumb people could be. It doesn't make any sense. All *that* for attention's sake.

People in my class do crazy things as well. Cadence always pulls boys' hair to get their attention. Max runs into girls on purpose in the hallway to get them to look up. I have seen classmates put things in Ms. Sempsrott's drink when she isn't looking and take on dares to do stuff when she *is* looking. I know people who have cheated on tests and started rumors that they couldn't take back. Some kids have tried to start fights while other kids have tried to end fights. Boys are always trying to talk cool and walk even cooler, while girls pretend to give them no attention. All the while, it is part of the girl's act to *get* attention. It's one big cycle, all in the name of popularity.

Popularity starts with people liking you. For people to like you, people have to notice you. For people to notice you, you usually have to do something to get their attention. Most of the time these things aren't good. It leaves people talking fake, walking fake, laughing fake, and acting fake all around.

Either you *used* to be popular, you *are* popular, or you are trying to *get* popular. If you don't belong to one of these groups, then you are left to the small number of outcasts, the untouchables. These are the humble, the honest, and the genuine. Or, in my case, the ones that get walked over, picked on, and laughed at. I know people say that you have to be yourself no matter what people think. I understand that, but that's much easier to talk about than to actually do.

I am convinced that's what those boys were doing when they stole my lunch—just trying to be popular. Trying to be important. Trying to belong. Trying to fit in. They are fitting in all right, but in the wrong set of clothes. My clothes fit just fine, so I have no problem staying me.

December 13, 2016:
Choosing Teams

I was leaning against the wall outside at recess today. Sometimes, I like to just sit in the shade and observe rather than participate. Mother told me once that too many people observe in life and not enough people participate, and that I needed to show more effort to do so. I think that she needs to show more effort not to be sad, but I would never, in my right mind, tell her that. She is my mother, and Pastor Scoggins says that we need to obey the people that are in charge over us. (Plus, I would probably get a bad spanking with the hickory switch if I did talk back to my mother like that.)

A few different classes were playing dodgeball, and they had chosen two captains to pick teams. It seems that recess is where legends are born, or at least boys my age seem to think so. One by one, people were chosen, until they all ran off to start the game. When the dust of kids cleared, there was only one girl left. She hung her head and slowly turned away.

I walked over and introduced myself. I told her that she could play on my team if she wanted to, and that's when she stopped crying. She had a pretty shirt with elephants on it. I liked it a lot, so I told her so. It's a shame to keep a compliment from someone who deserves it. It's cheating them out of a small blessing. She smiled and thanked me and told me that her name was Luciana.

I asked Luciana where she was from. She said that her country is directly below our country. She said that where she is from, they play soccer more than dodgeball and have big celebrations called fiestas. Come to find out, she lives right down the street from me with her mom, dad, and two sisters. It seems like I have gotten lucky this week because I have met two people who I think are very cool. I asked Luciana if we could be friends, and this made her smile again. I think that smiling is contagious, and it's amazing what little things can bring one on.

For the rest of recess, we played on the swings together and talked about everything we could think of. We kicked our legs forward, swung our heads back, and watched the sky rushing toward us. We laughed together, and for a short time, we forgot that there was such a thing as bullies and team captains. When the bell rang, I said goodbye to Luciana and went inside.

When school let out at 3:05, more big kids followed me into the bathroom. I knew that I was in trouble already, but there was no use running. They grabbed me and kicked open a stall door. Together, they lowered me into the toilet bowl. I thrashed wildly and tried to hold my breath, but soon I was forced to start drinking the water. I drank so much that my head got dizzy. Then, they flushed the water and pulled me out.

They pushed me to the ground. They told me that Luciana's family doesn't belong here and that they don't deserve the freedom that our country provides. They said that her father doesn't speak English and that people should speak our language if they want to live in our country. I started to tell them that Luciana spoke perfect English, but that would have just made them angrier. A flame added to another flame does nothing but make the fire grow bigger. That's what Uncle Billy once told me.

They started mocking me and calling me names (which I preferred over drinking toilet water, honestly). The boys urged me to fight back, but I didn't. They kicked me and walked out. Some boys were in the bathroom when it happened, but they washed their hands quietly and didn't look at me. After all, it wasn't them on the floor with wet hair, was it? Pastor Scoggins said that a man named Pilate once washed his hands after people wanted to kill Jesus because he didn't want Jesus' blood on him. Those boys must have not wanted any blood on their hands either. I guess I can't blame them.

December 17, 2016:
Tears

Tears are a strange thing. I used to think that there are only sad tears, like the tears that ran down Mother's cheeks on the day of the funeral—the last day that I saw Mother genuinely smile. That day, Uncle Billy had the same kind of tears in his eyes. Those tears seem to be the worst. They never run out and hurt just as bad each time they spill down your cheeks. But those aren't the only kind of tears.

One day at school, I saw Brett Jenkins get into a fight with Sawyer Crow over a piece of bubble gum. Brett is bigger than Sawyer, and Brett beat him up pretty good. Everyone was cheering and yelling before the fight was broken up. After the teachers pulled everyone apart, I saw the craziest thing. Sawyer was the one on the ground with blood coming from his nose, but Brett was the one crying! I couldn't get over it. Tears of anger are what they were. I learned that day that some tears force themselves out even when you don't want them to show up.

When I went to the theatre last month, I couldn't take my eyes off of this elderly couple. Their reactions to the movie were so interesting that I couldn't focus on the movie itself. In some scenes, the couple laughed so hard that they started crying and slapping each other's knees. In other scenes, the couple took out tissues to wipe their eyes because it was so sad. Just when I thought they couldn't cry anymore, they let loose again when the music started playing softly toward the end of the movie. I couldn't make up my mind if they were happy or sad or confused. I guess that tears can go from happy to sad to confused and back to happy again with the flip of a switch. Tears are funny that way.

Marla Purkett once asked Dane Wilson to be her boyfriend. He rejected her, which made her cry. Then, Dane turned around and started crying in the pickup line after school because his mom got mad at him and said that his dad would deal with him when they got home. I think it's amazing that we can make other people cry and other people can make us cry all in the same day.

People cry for all sorts of reasons. I know that much. I also know that there aren't any wasted tears. They all matter, including the tears that Luciana cried on the playground that day. I'm just glad that I was able to help change her tears. There is no greater feeling than removing bad tears and replacing them with good ones.

December 19, 2016:
Finding Blue

Ms. Sempsrott looked tired today. She kept taking her glasses off and rubbing her eyes. But it wasn't the kind of rub that said, "Something is in my eye." It was the kind of rub that said, "This day needs to end. And the next one. And the next one." I felt sorry for her. Right at that moment though, she looked up at me and showed me her smile-mask, and that made everything okay.

She gave us another writing assignment. This time, she said that she wanted us to pick any object in the room and write about it. Then, she sat back down and sighed loudly. It was the kind of sigh that makes your shoulders sink.

I liked the assignment, but I couldn't decide what to write about because there were too many things to choose from. It was a little bit frustrating to be honest. I gave a shoulder-sinking sigh myself and began fiddling with my shoe. That's when the idea hit me. I picked up my pencil and started writing . . .

> This is my shoe.
> It is dark navy blue.

I paused to think and looked at my shoe again. But this time, my pants caught my eye. They were blue as well! This didn't make any sense. I imagined my pants and my shoe battling against each other. My shoe was wearing an eye patch and my pants were wearing large golden earrings. Cannons fired in the background as they clashed their swords and fought over which one was the real *blue*. It made me smile, but it also made me think about life as well. I turned back to my paper . . .

> This is my shoe.
> It is dark navy blue.
> Wait, my pants are blue too.
> This cannot be true.
> Because if my shoe is blue, then can my pants claim it too?
> If I am me, and you are you,
> Then one of us is a pant, the other a shoe.
> So the only thing we can do is be our own blue.

This time, Ms. Sempsrott read my poem and started crying. I wasn't sure why at the time, but once I got home and thought about it, I figured it out. She is sad, and my poem made her even sadder. It wasn't my intention. All I was trying to say is that my pants and my shoe are different, so they both can't claim to be the same thing. Maybe she will be like the old couple at the theatre and turn her sad tears to happy tears. And maybe, just maybe, one day she will find out that she has a *blue* too. And that it's hers, and only hers. And that no one can take that away from her.

January 8, 2017:
The Boy with the Hat

Yesterday, Mother wanted me to run down to Bradburn's Grocery and pick up a loaf of bread. I was getting ready to walk into the store when I saw a boy fall while rollerblading. It looked like the bad kind of fall, the one where your leg burns for a few days and the red scab itches.

I felt sorry for the boy, so I ran over to see if he was all right. The hat that the boy had been wearing was lying on the ground a few feet away. I walked over and picked it up. It wasn't one like the boys around town wear at baseball games. This hat was round and square at the same time, and it didn't seem big enough for the boy's head. He seemed very embarrassed when I handed it back to him.

The boy said thanks but wouldn't look me in the eyes, as if he was ashamed or something. I smiled and asked if he was okay. He said that he was fine, but he didn't seem fine, so I asked again just to make sure. The boy was quiet for a moment, but then he started talking. He said that many kids had not been nice to him and that his family was not welcome in their neighborhood. It seemed like he needed to get some things off of his chest, so we went ahead and sat down on the sidewalk to talk for a few minutes. I knew that the bread could wait. Some things are just more important.

His family is from a country across the ocean. In his country, women cover their entire body except for their eyes, and men pray several times a day. I saw nothing wrong with the boy and didn't understand why kids would be mean to him. Just the other day I had prayed as well, so I didn't see anything wrong with praying either. He stuck out his hand to introduce himself. He said his name was Rasheed. I shook his hand in return and introduced myself. We talked a few more minutes, finally said goodbye, and went our separate ways.

I bought the bread, knelt down to pet a lady's dog, and then whistled my way back toward my apartment. I was almost home when some kids jumped out of the bushes in front of me. This has happened a lot lately, but it is the first time that it has happened outside of school. They formed a circle around me. They poked me in the shoulders, jeering and laughing. I didn't think the game was very funny. Then, one of the boys pushed me hard. I flew across the circle and landed in the arms of another boy. He shoved me back, and soon I was being thrown around the circle like a pinball. Finally, the punch came, and I fell to the ground. I saw blood dripping from my lip onto the pavement. I stood up the best I could before another boy punched me in the stomach. As I fell to the ground again, all of the boys started taking turns kicking me. They spit on me and ripped my shirt and threw my bread in the gutter. They told me to stay away from the boy with the hat. His family is dangerous, they said, and caused our country to go to war. They said that his family didn't believe like ours and that they deserved to be put in jail or killed. Boys have told me their opinions throughout the school year so far, and not to be stubborn, but I can't help but think that no one cares about their opinions! Just because several people believe in something doesn't make it right!

The boys left me lying on the ground and high-fived each other. They seemed proud of what they had done to me. I sat up and touched my lip. It felt like a hornet had stung it. I was pretty dirty, and a little bruised, but I seemed to be all right. I stood up, shook the dust out of my hair, and wiped the blood from my mouth again. Sometimes in life, all we can do is get back up and finish the journey home.

Thinking back, I realized that the neighbors saw the whole thing happen. When I looked at them, they went back inside and closed their door. Some people think it's easier to look the other way, I guess. No one else was around, and for a few moments things felt lonely. Very lonely. I slumped the rest of the way to our apartment and walked inside to change my clothes. I didn't bother telling Mother about it, but I did apologize for not getting the bread. (She didn't seem to care either way.) I feel better now that I have written about the whole incident, but yesterday was a rough day. Luckily, every day is a new day, which means we get the chance to wake up and start over.

March 7, 2017:
A New Nickname

A lot of the same stuff has continued throughout this spring. I make friends with the ones that no one else wants anything to do with, and afterwards, I pay for it. Sometimes, I have paid for it in stolen lunches and stolen snack money. Other times, I have paid for it with bruised ribs or split lips. It's never comfortable, and I never grow used to it. I am just never surprised anymore when it does happen.

I tried to tell the teachers a few times, but nothing was done about it. The kids who have bullied me the most are the ones that the teachers like the most. Those kids know how to tell the teachers what the teachers want to hear, and their parents believe them even more than the teachers do! It can be so frustrating.

Some kids have even started calling me by a new name: Colorblind. Sometimes, they call me that instead of my real name (even the kids that I have never had a problem with before). They usually do it when the teacher isn't around and no one can get them in trouble. I guess it shouldn't bother me much. After all, I prayed a few months ago to become colorblind, and now people are finally noticing. That's a good thing, right?

Prayer answered.

The way I see it, if they are focused on bullying me, then they *aren't* focused on the kids that they would normally be bullying. I don't mind being the focus of things if it keeps other people from being hurt. I just wish there were other people willing to do the same thing so that we could join up and face the bullies as a team. Either way, I believe in what I'm doing. Uncle Billy used to always say, "Your pain isn't being wasted as long as it's helping other people."

I haven't written anything in a while because sometimes my mind is too overwhelmed to think straight. I'm sorry if you read this and feel like I have left a few parts out. I have tried to record the highlights in this journal. Everything else that has happened this school year has just been a repeat of what I have already mentioned. But even though the bullying has been bad, and the kids doing the bullying have gotten meaner, I won't stop being kind. There is always hope in kindness. And sometimes, it only takes one kid to believe in a hope like that to start making a difference. Even ten year olds understand that.

March 14, 2017:
Scars Speak Louder than Words

S cars tell the real stories. Whether it's a small cut from falling on the playground or a missing arm from a war wound (like we saw on a video in history class last week), scars have a voice of their own. I think their stories are the most important ones because they are honest and true. In English class, we have been learning about autobiographies. Well, scars seem to write their own autobiographies, but in a much more meaningful way.

You can learn a lot about a person from their scars. Uncle Billy has scars on his knee from a surgery that he had his senior year of high school. Apparently, he was tackled blindside in the state play-offs. Mother has a scar on her chin where she crashed her bike when she was seven. Mr. Foran, our janitor at school, has a scar running down his palm from where he tried to get a fishhook out of a fish's mouth a few years back. Mrs. Dutchray, from across the street, said that she has scars on her chest where she fought, and beat, breast cancer. Even I have a scar above my left eyebrow where I slipped and hit my head on our coffee table when I was four. (Mother said that she passed out when she saw the blood, although I don't remember that part.)

Those aren't the only type of scars though. I once overheard Mother talking to Pastor Scoggins at church, and she told him that the Lord left scars on her heart from what happened that day at the stoplight. Maybe some scars are invisible, but does that mean that they hurt any less? Do those scars stay with you forever like the scars that you can see on your body? When I asked Uncle Billy, he said that some things left you scarred for life. We either let them heal or continue to notice them every day. For Mother, I guess time isn't a good enough medicine to heal her scars. Not yet, at least. I only hope that one day they will start to dim a little bit, or not be as noticeable. Then, I will get to see her smile again. She really does have a beautiful smile when it's genuine.

All scars are important—the good kind as well as the bad kind. They help us remember where we have come from, and in that way, they help direct us to where we need to go. I know that some people want to forget where they came from, but it doesn't make those memories any less important. If anything, it makes those memories more important. Ms. Sempsrott often tells us that everything we have done has made us into who we are today. I am starting to see what she means.

As my school year has grown longer, so has the history of my scars. Some are small, and some are large. Some are shallow, and some are deep. But they are all there, writing their autobiographies one line at a time. I don't know how the stories will turn out, but I do know that they will be something special. Because that's what happens when you pray, and that's what happens when you are kind, and that's what happens when you choose to dance when the clouds grow dark. The stories are always special.

April 21, 2017:
Sometimes We Just Know

So far, I have told my story in the best way I know how. It has been honest, and that's the best way to tell a story. It has also taken a lot of time and a lot of paper, and often my hand has hurt from writing so much. But I'm glad that I did it because someone out there needs to hear it. Maybe there are people out there who have a story similar to mine, and they need to know that they aren't alone!

Either way, this strange feeling has been creeping over me the last few days (maybe the last few weeks, but some parts have been a blur). It's hard to explain, but I guess it's the feeling you get on Sunday night when you know that it's almost time for school to start back on Monday. Or the feeling you get when your mother says that you only have one more hour left to play at the theme park. It's a sinking feeling, one that weighs on your shoulders and makes you feel like you are walking through thick mud. It's the feeling that time is running out. The feeling of leaving soon. The feeling of going on a permanent vacation where you say goodbye to everything that you know.

If the feeling is true, then I don't know how much time I'll have to write anymore. That may sound a little crazy, but sometimes we just know that something is going to happen. Not because someone tells us, or because we were given a sign, but because we just know. And all we can do when it does happen is try to be brave and remember who we are in that moment. So if my feeling is right and something does happen, then know that it has been a pleasure getting to share my story with you.

Part 2

The World of White

Chapter 1
What Others Were Doing

I t was a day that artists would have wanted to paint. Clouds formed shapes of appetizing desserts and drifted haphazardly across a baby blue sky. The sun couldn't be seen, but it could be felt, its light warm enough to leave the jacket at home but cool enough to demand a sweater. Leaves had turned shades of orange, red, and yellow. They speckled the sidewalks as well as the mountainsides, leaving patches of color across the landscapes in the distance. People flocked to the drive-in theatre, eager to enjoy the last few weekends before it closed for the season. Bonfires were lit, hot chocolate was stirred, and corn mazes were prepared. The world was at peace, the atmosphere draping its snug blanket across the earth's body.

John Mark's mother was at the Roses retail store buying him another boat that he could float merrily down the stream the next time it rained. Ms. Sempsrott was sitting on her couch sipping hot tea and brainstorming classroom activities for her students. "Cotton Top" Cody was playing video games while his dad sat in his office preparing a sermon for the following Sunday. Mrs. Cloggins, from 4B, was watering her plants while humming a song that her mother used to sing while tucking her into bed at night. The homeless man down the road was sitting by the green bench, wearing a new pair of thrown-out shoes that he had come upon. Mr. Perkins was delivering the mail and still wearing his smile-mask. "Nike Man" was running, "Sweet Tooth Nana" was eating, and "Ma'am Talk-A-Lot" was still waving her hand weights wildly in the air as she talked on her cell phone. The town kept its rhythm and danced to the beat of the world, and everyone carried their day in their pocket. That's the only thing that people wanted to do on a day that was perfect; a day that artists would have wanted to paint.

But while people smiled and laughed and hummed the earth's melody, something of much greater significance was happening. If you drive past the old Morganton Baptist Church and curve around Bradburn's Grocery, the road eventually forks off onto Hideaway Street. At the end of Hideaway Street, past the long row of charcoal apartments and the new bait shop, a crooked "Dead End" sign leans against a rusted, iron gate. Beyond that gate, over the pothole-infested hill, a field with jagged rows of tombstones lies dormant—all except for one. The one with a woman collapsed in front of it with the smell of "too much to drink" on her breath. At the very second that "Old Man" Riggins was playing another song on his weathered guitar and the "Rainbow Man" was painting another golden sunset, the wooden core of a woman's soul was splintering. While people were creating memories that they never wanted to forget, she was fighting memories that she never wanted to remember. For that is what her life had become, a memory that had overstayed its welcome.

Soon, the sun would set completely and the stars would awaken and the night would arrive at its scheduled time. Families would convene around dinner tables, and children would fight their parents about staying up late to watch one last TV show. Everyone would do something, following the pattern they had always followed; the pattern that they assumed was normal and would never be taken away. But for Laurie Vickers, the pattern would never be the same. The stars would never shine as bright, the moon would never appear as full, and the cry of a ten-year-old boy would never fade.

Chapter 2
Remembered

Laurie's entire body sat motionless except for one numb arm raised in front of her face. Slowly, deliberately, she traced the outline of each letter, allowing a new layer of dirt to cover her fingertip with each stroke. She had grown addicted to the grimy feel of earth on her hands, her cheeks, her eyelashes. It reminded her of her disgrace, the only thing that she could rely on to be a constant in her life.

She carried the look of an artist, scrutinizing every minute detail of the gravestone's canvas. It was death's masterpiece, *her* masterpiece, her life's work. Originally, the letters had mourned with her, bowing their heads respectfully and sharing in her grief. They had welcomed her, accepted her, and let her know that she wasn't the only mother who had lost her heart this way. After a few weeks, however, their attitude had changed. They grew impatient, annoyed, even angry. They began hinting that there was something that she could have done to prevent the tragedy. Something that she *should* have done. Finally, they had grown disgusted with her. They had let her know that her actions were unforgiveable. That *she* was unforgiveable. All they did now was remind her that her future was depleted and that her soul was damned. But she had accepted it, so her response never changed. She simply traced the letters and wept cold tears and watched through blurred vision as her son's memories replayed over, and over, and over again.

She didn't know how long she had sat there. She never did. The wind lashed out with its stinging fingers and wrapped her hair in a noose around her neck. It was nature's subtle way of telling her that she didn't have to live through the storm. That she could just end it. But hadn't the storm already arrived? Once you experience the storm inside your soul, you no longer have to fear the storm outside your body. It all seems senseless, hypnotic, futile. Nothing can harm you once you have experienced the agony of the soul. So there was nothing left to do but to continue to sketch the letters and numbers.

Royce Chandler Vickers
October 25, 2006–April 24, 2017

Laurie knew she shouldn't have come. Not on this day. Not on the day that Royce would have turned eleven. She had sworn that she wouldn't come, that it was too difficult, that it was too painful; but here she was, in the same position that she had been every day since his funeral.

She let her hand fall away and fumbled for the bag that lay beside her. Only two items were in it: a quart of birthday cake flavored ice cream (Royce's favorite) and a bottle of Irish Fire Whiskey (her favorite). She no longer bothered hiding the alcohol in a brown paper bag. It didn't matter who saw it or what they thought about it. Her shame was beyond the point of embarrassment anyway. Royce was gone, and he was the only one that had mattered.

Yanking off the ice cream lid, Laurie mechanically dipped a plastic spoon into the cup. She smelled the spoon before taking her first bite, just like Royce had always done. She once asked him why he did that.

"Because, Mom, it always reminds me of warm memories . . . which is odd because ice cream is always cold!"

His voice was there, happy and pleasant and passionate. Everything she wasn't.

She only lasted a few bites before her stomach grew tense, and the tears began to fall. It had definitely been a bad idea coming on this day.

The bottle.

She needed the bottle.

Laurie tossed the yellow ice cream cup to the ground and replaced it with a tear-drop shaped bottle containing amber liquid. She tore off the plastic wrapper as if it was her own birthday and the long-awaited time to open gifts had finally arrived. In a way, it was a gift to herself (the same gift that she bought herself every day but was no less special). It wrapped its comforting arms around her shoulders and soothed her fragile nerves. *There, there, Laurie. I'm here, my love . . .*

With shaking hands, she brought the bottle to her lips and drank as much as she could before half-spitting, half-coughing the bottle away from her mouth. It burned down her throat and deep into her chest. The first sips always burned, but she liked that. It was yet another small way to punish herself.

She wiped her mouth and stared at the tombstone that was staring back at her. A gust of wind slapped her face. It was bullying her, taunting her. She clenched her teeth in hate, not at the wind, but at herself. For holding onto herself but letting Royce go—for *choosing* to let him go. The wind and the letters were right. It was her fault, and that would never change. She would have to live with that every day. The wind howled in agreement. She took another deep swig, swallowing it quickly.

A shadow fell over her, as if someone had walked up behind her and blocked out the sun. She looked up. Something had blocked the sun, but thankfully she was still alone. Clouds that had been creamy white earlier in the evening had now turned ashy grey. The weather was intruding. This was her time to celebrate his day, and she deserved an ounce of relief for it. Had the weather no respect for her suffering? She raised the bottle again, this time swishing it around to let the fire touch all sides of her mouth before swallowing.

She turned her attention back to the stone and began tracing the last lines. The ones that she always started but could never quite finish . . .

"He danced when the clouds were dark, sang when the storm was loud, and loved when others lost sight. This love will always be remembered."

"Remembered." Laurie whispered it as if she was telling the air a secret that she didn't want the wind to overhear. The word is only as good, or as bad, as the person who gives it a voice. And Royce's voice had been loud.

She thought about why Royce would be remembered. He was a blessing to everyone who knew him. He was a heated blanket in an icy breeze, a tall glass of cold water on a scorching day, a fireplace to warm numb hands, a revitalizing cure for the wounded spirit. He simply loved people. Anyone could see his energy, his laughter, and his enthusiasm for the details of life. His passion was contagious.

And it wasn't just a mother glorifying her own child. Laurie thought about the day of his funeral and how so many people had shown up to pay their respects. Even the homeless man from the green bench had laid a fake flower at Royce's feet. Laurie had always heard that if you wanted to find out who loved people, then ask the homeless and they would tell you. Classmates, church friends, neighbors, family—all there for one purpose: to remember Royce. He had accepted the world, but the world had refused to accept him.

As the minutes passed and the bottle ran dry, Laurie couldn't trace the letters anymore because they kept shifting. Maybe she was the one that was shifting, but she couldn't tell. Finally, she gave up and dropped her hand into her lap. Tears welled in her eyes again. She once thought someone could run out of tears, but she was discovering that she had an endless reservoir. Sometimes, tears are the only answer that satisfied the soul.

A raindrop hit her face and quickly fell in line with the other tears that had started marching down her cheek. She looked to the sky. There were only black clouds above her now, offering neither sympathy nor rest. Lightning flashed in the distance. She closed her eyes as water began falling in quick spurts, the droplets softly pelting her skin. Her brother Billy used to always spread his arms and smile at the sky. He genuinely believed that the rain could wash him clean.

Laurie wished that she could believe like that, but as she closed her eyes, there was no healing that took place. All she saw was Royce staring back at her, tear stains coursing down his cheeks as well. They were tears that she had caused.

Gathering the last bit of emotion that she could muster, Laurie threw the bottle, shattering it against a tombstone a few feet away. She ripped at the grass and screamed at the rain until her voice went hoarse. Then, she collapsed on the ground with her body heaving, longing for another drink and one second of release from the ghosts that haunted her.

Chapter 3
Our Ghosts

W e all have ghosts. Some loom larger than others, and some are disguised better than others, but they all exist. They linger deep within our thoughts, waiting to be called on stage to present their act in front of a deteriorating mind. And most of the time, they get applauded back on stage for an encore. Laurie knew that she couldn't leave the theatre. At this point, she would settle for a seat on the back row, but that too, seemed impossible.

She had many ghosts, all of which tortured her in a way that almost made them feel sorry for her. *Almost.* Since Royce had died, all of Laurie's ghosts had begun resurfacing again, even the ones that she had kept buried for years. They all rose within her, wearing different masks. Perhaps, that was the hardest part of all—trying to decide which ghost, from which time, could cause the most harm.

They invaded her senses like a conquering army. They wore a Spider-Man backpack, an elegant evening gown, and a beer-stained T-shirt. They sounded like the theme song of *Power Rangers*, the tapping of raindrops on a windshield, and the screeching of sliding tires. They smelled like stale cigarette smoke, "too much to drink" on the carpet, and expensive cologne. They tasted like a four-course meal, a Lunchables snack pack, and a flat Coke. They felt like chin scruff rubbing against her cheek, glass slicing through her skin, and blood oozing down her forehead. They were all different, and yet all the same—each one more dangerous than the last. The past never *really* stayed in the past, did it? But how do you stop that? How do you cope with that?

Others around her had battled their own ghosts in the attempt to win back territory they had lost. Across the street, John Mark's mother fought her ghosts by smoking cigarettes on the porch while she read old letters when no one else was home. "Old Man" Riggins, Laurie's neighbor on the left, battled his ghosts by placing flowers at a roadside grave marker once a week. Laurie's father-in-law, Grandpa Don, had ghosts as old as the Second World War. He wrestled his ghosts by calling his fellow ex-marines in the middle of the night to ask if they ever regretted what they had done to people during the war. All were real people with real struggles, grappling with human resolve to try and find purpose in a better tomorrow—to try and find a *reason* to hope in a better tomorrow. What Laurie found more disturbing than the actual existence of the ghosts was the idea that they had found a permanent residence in her mind. To think that they might never move out was a suffocating thought. And even though she knew those types of thoughts were like admitting defeat, she couldn't help but detect a sense of finality in them.

"Fear is not of the spirit, but of the flesh," Pastor Scoggins had once said. "We can choose to not accept it. We can choose to overcome evil with good."

That was the last sermon that Laurie had heard and the last Sunday that she had seen the inside of a church building. The following day had been *the* day—the last day that she had genuinely smiled.

Pastor Scoggins believed that overcoming fear and guilt was a choice, but Laurie had not handled decisions too well in the last two-and-a-half years. The road to recovery was twisted in knots. It seemed like her circumstance would never change, especially now that she felt responsible for so much hurt. She knew that her ghosts feasted on this insecurity, and for the time being, she could do nothing else but offer them seconds. She knew that she needed to resist, but her strength, mentally as well as physically, was running low. Her ghosts were indulging on the leftovers of her soul. And if they ate too long, she knew that they might not only win the battle, but win the war.

Chapter 4
The Pact between Demons and Men

Later that night, Laurie shut her eyes, but no sleep came. It had been like this ever since Royce's funeral. She slept little, and when she did, her sleep was full of fidgeting and night terrors and waking up in sweat-soaked shirts. The only remedy was the bottle, which her ghosts particularly loved. It was the only thing that silenced them. If they had whiskey pouring down their throats, then they didn't have a voice to scream in her head. So each time she woke with ghosts crying for her attention, she gave them what they wanted and fed them, just as a mother would feed her newborn child. They always held up their end of the bargain and shut their mouths, allowing her dreamless sleep. It was the least they could do. There should be no pacts between demons and men, but Laurie had found one she thought she could be at peace with.

Alcohol had always been a part of Laurie's life, like a birthmark or a childhood keepsake. She was given her first drink when she was four years old. She remembered that moment because she had loved the blue and red colors glistening off of the can. She had outstretched her curious arms toward the table, and instead of pushing her hands away, Laurie's father had scooted the can within her reach. He had laughed at the look on Laurie's face as she crinkled her nose and spit out the unwelcome taste. At some point, unwelcome tastes can become very welcome tastes with the right motivation. The taste had now become her best friend, making itself at home in the spare bedroom of her heart. It had become a part of her.

People drink for many reasons, and Laurie was no different. That's how she justified the habit. Justifications are always on standby, waiting to board the plane of your reasoning. Mrs. Dorene, from 2C, always drank to ease her anxiety after reading disturbing news in the paper about another terrorist bombing. Laurie's cousin, Marcy, drank every time she hosted a girl's night because she said it would be snobbish to host an event and not participate in the entertainment. Laurie's brother, Billy, drank when he watched football because he claimed that beer always went better with pizza. (Plus, he said it helped take the edge off of his anger when his team was struggling.) Laurie's mailman, Mr. Perkins, drank when his route was finished because he had been chased by dogs all day and needed to relax. Miss Jane, Laurie's neighbor on the right, drank when she watched her crime mysteries in order to help her get in the mind-set of the killer.

As for Laurie? Well, one could say she drank because of Royce, or because of *the* funeral, or because she felt empty, or guilty, or lost, and all of those would have been correct; but beyond all that, at her most vulnerable core, Laurie knew she drank because it was the only time she could make herself forget that she didn't belong. It was the only time she could make herself forget that the world really was as nasty as it appeared to be.

Alcohol helped dull her heartache and numb her pain. It could even help make her pain disappear completely if it was given enough time and energy. She would do anything for a moment of temporary relief, even if that meant waking up hours later with the same sharp depression rotting her conscience. To Laurie, that moment of peace was like a cold drop of water landing on hot coals. Her cold water came in the form of Irish whiskey. Each drop was more soothing than the last. She had found something that she loved, or rather, something that loved her. And like a marriage, she had gotten to the point where she couldn't see life *without* the bottle. It seemed they were bonded for eternity.

What was alcohol? It was Laurie's saving grace.

Chapter 5
Bad Things and Broken Pieces

L aurie heard knocking in her dreams for five minutes before she realized it was real. She rolled out of bed, knocked a bottle aside, and stumbled down the stairs. Everything was *too*—the morning was *too* early, the light was *too* bright, and her stomach was *too* upset.

She pulled the door open a pinch. Billy was waiting patiently and holding up a cup of coffee as an offering. She knew that he had come to try and cheer her up. She wasn't in the mood to see anyone, as usual, but she would never turn away her brother. She unlocked the chain and left the door ajar. Billy walked in, handed her the coffee, and kissed her on the cheek. She turned around with no kiss in return and shuffled into the kitchen. Billy made himself comfortable on the couch, kicking his feet up on the armrest.

"How is my younger sister doing?" he called after her.

Laurie peeked around the corner at him and narrowed her already squinting eyebrows. "Umm, same as she was yesterday, and the day before that, and the day before that." She took down a flask from the cabinet and unscrewed the top. Pouring what was left from the stainless steel container, she tossed it on the counter without bothering to put the top back on.

Billy listened, aware of what she was doing, but remained quiet. Sometimes there is more comfort in our silence than in our words. He knew which time this called for. Laurie walked back into the living room and sat in the recliner across the room. Billy smiled pleasantly without any expectation of a smile in return, and he didn't get one.

"Talked to Mr. Falkirk down at the bakery when I was picking up the coffee," Billy said, breaking the lingering silence. "He said that Pastor Scoggins was helping him put together a bake sale for Ms. Durian's granddaughter. Apparently, the hospital bills have gotten out of control a bit. Caught the family in a bind. I thought it was a nice gesture to get the whole church involved."

Laurie offered a robotic nod and sipped her drink. The sharp smell of whiskey wafted from her cup, infecting the air like a disease. She stared into space, the only place her mind felt at home. Billy acted like it didn't bother him (which it did) and that he had seen it all before (which he had). He continued talking, more to himself than to Laurie. "I also saw that they are putting in another Wendy's down the road. That will be much more convenie—"

"Why are you here, Billy?" Laurie interrupted. Her eyes bore a deep hurt, but not from his words. He was only trying to do what big brothers do best. She knew that, but it was still too sensitive for her. Averting an issue makes the air even heavier, and the air in her life was already crushing.

Laurie looked at the Styrofoam cup in her hands, which was shaking ever so lightly. It reminded her of when her mom had begun dealing with the onset of Parkinson's. Initially, the disease had only effected one side of her mother's body. The tremors had started in her left arm and were only apparent at specific times—like when her arm was resting still on the couch, or when she was trying to poke thread through a needle before sewing, or when she was holding a mug in her lap with hot tea in it—gentle, methodical shaking that never slowed down. The sound of her brother's voice snapped her eyes forward once more.

"I just wanted to see you," Billy said. "Worried about my sister, that's all. Thought you could use seeing a friendly face."

"I appreciate it, but I need more than a friendly face." She took another gulp of coffee and frowned at the strength of it. It wasn't strong *enough*.

"It's time we start getting you some help," Billy insisted, "before I have to watch another family member get buried."

Laurie recoiled, as if sprayed with ice-cold water. A bitter glare contorted her face. Through gritted teeth, she said, "You want to help, Billy? Then answer me this—why do bad things happen to good people?" Tears quickly rose to the corners of her eyes, but dwindled, refusing to spill over just yet.

Billy's shoulders sank. "That was a little abrupt. I'm sorry. We don't have to get into this if you don't want to, Laurie. It's just . . . I'm concerned about you. I just wanted to check on—"

"Well, we are here, aren't we? Talking about it already? So help me understand that. It should be simple for a church-going person who hasn't lost their faith yet." She hadn't intentionally meant to hurt him, but she knew that the comment had stung. It wasn't his fault that her faith had been broken.

"I don't have a good answer for you, Laurie. I'm sorry." He let out a long sigh, his demeanor suddenly fatigued. He hesitated for a brief moment, then spoke. "I mean—" but again, he stopped short and shook his head, as if what he was about to say didn't matter anymore.

"You mean what?" Laurie demanded.

Billy shrugged. "I mean, there's no good answer to that question without faith," he said. "It's impossible to answer it without at least *some* level of belief in a higher power. You and me, we just see things differently, and nothing I can say will make you feel better or change your opinion right now. It's obvious that you aren't quite ready to have those discussions yet, and that's fine. The time will come."

"Don't let that stop you," Laurie said. "Go ahead and try. At this point, my faith can't get any lower anyway." She drank more coffee and situated herself in the recliner. She felt her head growing warmer, unsure if it was from her anger, last night's hangover, or the spiked coffee. Most likely a combination of all three. "Well go on," she insisted.

Billy's eyes searched her carefully, unsure of the ground he was about to walk. They had gotten into discussions before, and the talks had never ended well. He had perhaps tried to push the issue too

70

quickly, before she had been given adequate time to get back on her feet—not that any time is adequate after you have lost a child. It had been weeks since he had last spoken to Laurie about her condition. When it worsened, he knew that he couldn't sit back and watch her deteriorate. He had to do *something*, which is why he was sitting in her living room now.

He took a deep breath, exhaled, and began, "Well, maybe you're seeing it from the wrong perspective." Laurie looked stupefied at him. He quickly continued before she could interject. "I know what you're saying when you say that bad things happen to good people, but I think that phrase alone implies that we are judging what is a *bad* thing and who is a *good* person. God doesn't see the world as we see it, so as long as we insist on seeing it our way, then we will continue to judge things as good or bad, as fair or unfair. And isn't that the real issue? When we say that bad things happen to us, what we really mean is that we didn't *deserve* to have those things happen to us. That it wasn't *fair*. It's almost as if we believe that we are entitled to have good things happen to us. I just don't think that's right. I don't think that's how God's mind works."

"Then how does it work?" Laurie said, her voice hardening.

Billy stood up and began pacing the room in concentration. "I think God created a beautiful world, but we chose to let sin corrupt it. Because of that, everything that he intends for good, Satan intends for evil. I think that God is the only one that can take the broken world we live in and mend it back together to form a beautiful masterpiece. I think that's our only hope, to believe that God sees history from start to finish and is still in control. To see that there is meaning and purpose in our suffering. To see that God is taking the mess in our lives and shaping it into something amazing."

"And just what possibly could be *amazing* about my life?" Laurie spat the line with biting sarcasm, already annoyed at the mention of God's purpose. She shook her head and looked at the ground. "There is nothing amazing about what has happened to me."

Billy eased back onto the couch. "Your life is amazing, because when you come through all of this heartache, you will be unstoppable. We just have to get you to the point where you stop blaming

God for what you have lost and start thanking God for what you have gained." Billy reached out to touch her arm, but she jerked it away, spilling coffee on her already-stained T-shirt. If it burned her, she showed no sign of pain.

"You can believe like that, Billy, but I can't! Not yet. I have tried, but I can't . . . and I'm *sorry.*" Laurie rose from the recliner and threw her cup in the kitchen sink. Then, she leaned against the counter and put her hands in her face.

Billy stood up and walked to the door. "It might do you some good to go see Pastor Scoggins tomorrow. I know it's the last place that you want to be, but sometimes the most unexpected blessings can come from the most unexpected places. In your case, that would be church." He opened the door and looked back at her one last time. "I know you don't believe, but I still do. Just don't close your heart to the possibility of hope. I'm here for you. That won't change. I love you, Sis."

He walked out to the sound of Laurie weeping.

Chapter 6
God Has Alzheimer's

Laurie had walked into Cornerstone Faith Assembly with her makeup strewn and her hair haphazardly swept to the side. She had no one to impress and hadn't been looking for anyone to impress her (not that anyone would have given her a second glance anyway in her condition). She hadn't really known why she had come, other than it was something to do, and Billy seemed to think it would help. She often acted like she ignored his advice, although inwardly, she knew he was right.

Now, she found herself in the back row, the last seat in the pew next to the wall. The fewer eyes she could avoid, the better. It was not quite halfway through the sermon, and already she wished that she could leave without Pastor Scoggins noticing. Today's sermon dealt with something concerning the patience of Joseph, but Laurie had lost focus. It was hard to concentrate when the face of your "would have been eleven-year-old son" kept popping up in every shadow.

The church was full of shadows, and thus, full of Royce. He had loved everything about the church, from Sunday school to local mission trips to Vacation Bible School to Pastor Scoggins. He often went over to play with the pastor's son, Cody, on Sunday afternoons. The pastor's family lived just outside of town in a log cabin in the mountains. Royce loved it because he said they owned "everything"—gadgets, games, four-wheelers—all the things that Royce would never have gotten to play with in his own home. Cody now sat on the front row with Royce's ghost sitting contently beside him. The ghost was constantly looking over his shoulder at Laurie, waving and offering his handsome smile. There were too many memories of her son in this place.

Laurie stood up and walked out.

She didn't care if the pastor saw her. She didn't care if the church members heard her. She especially didn't care if God frowned upon her. They could deal with it in their own way. After all, she hadn't come here for them. She had come for . . . well, she wasn't quite sure.

She marched down the steps of the small building and sat on a bench that rested under an oak tree beside the parking lot. The breeze was nice, and the air felt cool on her aching forehead. Déjà vu engulfed her as she realized it wasn't the first time that she had been under this tree. She turned around, half-expecting to see Royce's dad laughing at her while they leaned against the tree trunk and watched Royce participate in an Easter egg hunt. That had been an amazing day. Afterward, they had gone to get ice cream and watched a movie at the house. Royce had fallen asleep in his father's lap while Laurie had fallen asleep against his shoulder. A gust of wind blew leaves across her feet, making her blink. Only aged roots and packed dirt stared up at her now. She looked back at the church.

Inside, she could hear the congregation singing "The Old Rugged Cross" for the benediction. Moments later, the church doors burst open, and kids poured down the front steps. Their shirts were already untucked and their ties askew. Royce's ghost ran behind them, squealing with laughter. Laurie crammed her eyes shut and took a few deep, methodical breaths. When she began to hear adult voices having adult conversations, she opened her eyes again. Men chatted and laughed energetically while women offered kind hugs to each other. There was no trace of Royce anywhere.

The person she was waiting on soon appeared at the top of the steps, shaking hands with each member that walked out of the building. It seemed to take much longer than it should have taken, but the crowed finally dispersed, and the parking lot emptied. As Laurie rose from the bench, Pastor Scoggins turned and smiled at her from the bottom step. It appeared that he had known she was there all along.

It was too late to turn back, so Laurie made her way over the steps and greeted the beaming pastor. "Pastor Scoggins," she said plainly.

"Laurie! It's so good to see you! Come here and let me get a look at you." He ushered her closer and gave her a small hug. Easing away, he smiled at her and tried to ignore the discouragement that clouded her eyes. He hesitated for a brief moment, but when Laurie remained silent, he continued talking. "How are you doing? Sherryl asked about you the other day and wanted to invite you over for dinner. She'll be glad that I ran into you."

"I appreciate that, but I'll respectfully decline," Laurie said. There was no resentment in her voice, just a statement of fact.

Pastor Scoggins recognized the gesture and nodded politely. "Well, the offer is always open, I can assure you of that." He smiled at her again.

She looked around the parking lot, as if she was impatiently waiting on someone to arrive. Pastor Scoggins once again eased the tension, trying to keep the atmosphere positive. "Really, I'm so glad you are here. It was an unexpected blessing. I know that the last few months haven't been easy. Healing takes time, I understand. We haven't wanted to pressure you, but know that we have been praying for—"

"I think that God has forgotten about me." She cut him off as she had cut off Billy. Averting his gaze, she cast her eyes downward and watched the toe of her shoe fumble with gravel from the parking lot. "I feel like God has Alzheimer's or something. People can cry out to him, they beg for healing, they remain faithful through it all and . . . nothing. It's like he forgets about them. As if he listens to their prayers but walks away and forgets they ever prayed. He forgets that there are people who need him in ways that only he can help." Laurie kicked at the rocks harder as she spoke, as if to emphasize each point. "I mean, think about the verses—God will give us the desires of our hearts and whatever we ask for in his name we will receive and blessed are those who mourn, for they will be comforted . . . all meant to inspire hope and to bring peace, but in reality, they're all just empty promises. They're pointless. It's like he forgot that he ever made them. Maybe God is the one with the mental disease, not us."

"Oh, Laurie, you know that isn't true," said Pastor Scoggins. "Even some of the most faithful men in the Bible experienced spiritually barren times in their lives. Times where they questioned if God even heard their cries. Times where they felt alone and afraid and angry. They felt forgotten as well. But in every situation, they learned lessons about God's sovereignty. They were reminded that God's ways aren't our ways, and our ways—"

"Aren't God's ways. I know that," Laurie replied flatly.

"Just because we don't always feel God, doesn't mean that he isn't there." Pastor Scoggins's voice was reassuring, but it was obvious that he felt anxious on her behalf. He sighed and put his hand on her elbow. "What matters is not how we enter *into* those times, but how we emerge *from* those times."

"Well, then answer me this," said Laurie quickly. "Does God deliberately allow Satan to bring ruin on us? Or allow pain to destroy our lives?" She was fighting back tears as she had too many times before. They were tears of bitterness and defeat. She clenched her jaw to try and maintain her composure. "Because if God hasn't forgotten us, then it must be that he simply doesn't care."

Pastor Scoggins took a deep breath and let it out slowly. "I don't have all the answers, Laurie. No pastor does. The issue of pain is always a difficult and complicated topic to discuss because there are no easy answers. At its core, I think sin has corrupted the world, and corrupt people make corrupt decisions. Because of sin, any chance we have at living a pain-free life has been erased. Everybody experiences some level of pain in their lives, whether it is directly linked to a choice they made or a choice that someone else made. Our choices have consequences, both good and bad. That's the tragedy and beauty of having free will."

Pastor Scoggins paused to see if Laurie would comment, but she remained motionless, staring at the ground. After a few seconds, he continued. "But it sounds like what you are really wondering is if God ever has an impure motive. And in that case, no, I don't believe his motives are flawed. God's only motive for us is love. Now, do I believe that sometimes God chooses to allow us to experience pain rather than removing it? Absolutely. But that too is driven by love. The Bible is full of stories where God used pain to fulfill his purpose."

"Well, the way I see it," Laurie interjected, "if God could prevent things from happening but chooses not to, then he is still to blame."

"That's because we can't see the full picture. God sees the entire history of the universe in a single spectrum, from the moment he spoke light into existence until the very second he returns. We only see a snapshot, a mere glimpse. You may not understand the plot of a novel while you are reading it, and how could you? You didn't write the story. But the author knows the outcome because he is the creator of it. Every detail, every action, and every character was written with a specific purpose in mind."

Laurie once again fiddled with the gravel and swatted away a tear that was crawling down her cheek. None of these things were things she wanted to hear, but somehow she knew it was the answer she would get. That was always the answer—God's purpose, everything happens for a reason, just have to have faith. Was there really no better solution?

Pastor Scoggins pointed back toward the church. "A few months ago, there was a boy in our church named R.J. I'm not sure if you remember him, but he experienced a terrible tragedy as well. At the time, he felt some of the same emotions that you are feeling. He was confused and upset and bitter. But if you talk to him now, his testimony is amazing! Not because of what happened *to* him, but because of what God did *through* him. He could have seen it as God destroying his life, but he chose to see it as God redeeming his life. And what about Job from the Bible? His faith was being tested beyond anything that he had ever experienced. Job had no way of seeing the blessing that lay before him at the time of his misery, but God knew the reward for remaining faithful."

Laurie quit playing with the gravel and glared at the pastor. "Well, I'm not into games. You have said before that God's timing is always perfect . . . that God is seldom early, but he's never late . . . but Royce is dead, and he isn't coming back. That means that God refused to answer." Another tear fell from her face.

Pastor Scoggins cleared his throat, trying to speak tenderly. "When John the Baptist was in prison, he too felt like Jesus could have done something to help his situation. He felt so frustrated that he even sent messengers to ask Jesus if Jesus really was who he claimed to be. But instead of saving John, Jesus sent word back simply explaining the miracles that God was performing outside the prison walls. In other words, Jesus was letting John know that, despite John's circumstances, God's glory was still being furthered in ways that John couldn't understand. We don't know how John reacted to this news, but it's a lesson that we can draw inspiration from today. I know that referring to a lot of old Bible stories probably won't help, but here is the point—God never acts unintentionally. He always answers prayers, although his answers are filtered through what will bring him the most glory. It's all a part of his bigger plan."

"But what does that mean for me then?" Laurie demanded. "Now that Royce is gone? I simply have to accept the fact that it's God's plan? That's it?" She was crying harder now, aware of the breakdown that was approaching. She was also aware that she didn't care. It was her time to be bitter.

"God will do anything for his glory," said Pastor Scoggins. "Even if that means orchestrating life through death." Laurie stopped sniffling and stared up at the pastor. The muscles in her jaws tightened. "He knows that sometimes the only way to save a life is—"

But Laurie didn't let him finish. She erupted, each word growing in intensity. "What life are you talking about? Royce was a good boy! He didn't *need* saving! He loved people, and he loved Jesus, and he was too young to be taken. Are you saying God brought Royce death because that was the only thing that would save him? I WON'T ACCEPT THAT! I WON'T!"

"That's not what I meant," Pastor Scoggins said, trying to calm Laurie down. "That wasn't what I was referring to. Let me expl—"

"NO!" Laurie screamed. "I don't need to hear any more. I'm done." She turned to walk away. That's why she never should have come. Talking about God did nothing but remind her that something should have been done to save her boy and that God was to blame for that *something*.

She cursed under her breath as she marched toward her car.

As she reached for her door handle, Pastor Scoggins called out to her. "Laurie, why are you here?"

"What?" she replied angrily, not even bothering to turn back around. "Why am I *here*? Did you really just ask that?"

"Yes," he replied. His voice was fatigued. "Taking your anger out on me isn't going to relieve the pain. I'm not the one that you need to fight. And I'm sorry, I truly am. I would gladly do everything that I could to take the pain away, but the battle isn't with me." Pastor Scoggins pointed to the sky. "It's with *him*."

Laurie scoffed. "Right. Battle with God . . . because that's worked every other time."

Pastor Scoggins insisted, "But have you really fought, or have you let bitterness steal your strength? I told you that I don't have the answers, but he does. Go home, get on your knees, and . . . well, fight in the trenches. Let him see your bitterness. Hold nothing back. In the end, it's not about winning and losing. It's about living free. And God *is* trying to set you free. You just don't realize it yet." He turned to walk away with Laurie still holding on to the handle of her car.

She pulled open the door and sank into the driver's seat. Battle it out with God? What good would it do to fight with someone who doesn't change his mind? She started the car and swerved onto the road.

"Fight in the trenches," she said out loud. "If that's what the pastor wants, then sure, that's what he'll get. All that it will do is lead to more pain. He'll see." The car's engine roared in agreement as she sped toward her apartment.

Chapter 7
The Battle

L aurie pulled into the parking lot of her apartment complex. She got out of the car and slammed the door shut, still fuming from her conversation with Pastor Scoggins. The "cool down" ride home had not helped. Having time to brood on the "should have saids" and the "what you don't understands" did nothing but further her rage.

She slowed her walk as she mounted the concrete steps that led to her front door. A memory flashed in front of her, sending waves of nausea through her stomach. Nearly three years ago, she had been standing on the same step talking to Billy after *the* funeral. Billy had made a similar comment about God that Pastor Scoggins had made—something about God allowing trials in our lives. Staring at an empty walkway, Laurie could still hear her shrill voice from so many months before, lashing out at her brother: "He is just sitting up there watching all of this happen, and we have to be the ones to pick up the broken pieces!" She could still see the hurt in Billy's demeanor. He had tried so hard to comfort her then, just as he had when he had brought her coffee the day before. She clenched her jaw and marched through the ghost of the memory, carrying some of its residue on her shoulders as she reached her door.

Once inside, she threw her keys on the couch and wasted no time making her way up the stairs. She paused at the top of the landing, but instead of walking into her own room, she pushed open Royce's door. His presence swept over her like a tidal wave. His room was just as he had left it, except that she had made his bed and arranged his stuffed animal pillows neatly on top. She walked over to his nightstand and picked up a picture that rested on it. The picture showed Royce, Billy, and herself on Royce's eighth birthday. Royce was wearing a *Power Rangers* T-shirt and holding up a Green Ranger action figure that he had gotten as a present. All three of them were smiling heartily. He had loved that day so much.

Laurie forced her eyes away from the picture and placed it back on the table where it belonged. She tried to convince herself that she was not here to reminisce, although she knew that would be a lie. She couldn't *not* reminisce. She never stopped thinking about Royce—his laughter, his joy, his *pain*—which brought her back to why she had come home. Pastor Scoggins wanted her to battle things out with God, and that's exactly what she intended to do. It was more to spite him than to actually receive answers. She knew there were no answers left. Her boy was gone.

She couldn't remember the last time that she had prayed (at least, the last time she had prayed a sincere prayer). In the last couple of years, she had found that the prayers she prayed far outweighed the answers she received. That combination had further led her to believe that either God had stopped listening, that he was listening but didn't care, or that that he had listened but had forgotten. Why would things change now? She didn't have to put up with stupidity like that all over again. Why waste her time? It was her time to vent, her time to release.

The last thing she wanted to do was pray. Even though she was completely alone, she still felt like she was giving in to all the people who said that prayer would work. She felt guilty at the thought of entertaining their suggestions, their kind words, their sympathy. It felt like she was betraying herself, like she was betraying the demons inside her who craved for her downfall. Then again, what other option did she have? There was nothing left of her *to* defeat. And just because she was going to pray didn't mean that it had to be long, or reverent, or genuine. Pastor Scoggins had said to be honest, so she would hold nothing back.

Laurie dropped to her hands and knees. It was the same position that Royce's dad used to get in when Royce wanted to ride on his back. Cold chills shivered across her body at the recollection of the memory.

She glanced out the window in front of her, unaware that just a few months earlier Royce had knelt at the same window while praying to the sky outside. *I pray I may, I pray I might, become colorblind and be given new sight.* The last light of the setting sun was on the horizon, casting a narrow strip of orange tint across the tree line. A few speckled stars had already begun to show themselves.

Laurie shut her eyes. She inhaled deeply through her nose, held it for a few seconds, and let the air rush out of her mouth. She did her best to calm her mind, although her hands had already begun to shake. There was nothing else to do but to get on with it. She drew another breath and opened her mouth to speak.

No sound came out.

In that moment, she realized that she had no idea what she wanted to say. When she was talking to Pastor Scoggins, or Billy, or any other person attempting to console her, she was bursting with things to shout at them. But now, now that she was finally in a place where she could unleash every thought and feeling, her words escaped her. It made the situation that much more annoying.

Her jaws opened wider but once again snapped close.

Why? Why couldn't she do it? Why did she feel so defeated? Laurie turned and looked at the birthday picture of Royce on the nightstand. His eyes pierced through hers, challenging her, begging her, hating her.

She tore her glance away and stared at the carpet, ashamed. She was sick of being ashamed. She was sick of being broken. She was sick of being tortured. She was sick of . . . *being!* Emotions provided the voice that her words could not. In an instant, the dam of her anger, her bitterness, and her hurt burst open, flooding the room in one giant sweep. Her face slumped forward until her forehead touched the floor, and her entire body began to heave. Her hands clutched the carpet, her fingers digging in as deep as they could to try and rip it out. She screamed because she couldn't speak, she cried because she couldn't laugh, and she sat on her knees because life wouldn't let her stand to her feet. All she could do was beat the ground harder and harder and hope that the screams of pain would suffice for a prayer.

Royce's face was everywhere: the floor, the wallpaper, the bookshelf, the lampshade, the nightlight. His singing saturated the air, and his dancing crammed the empty space around her. Laurie couldn't escape, couldn't run away. As her crying grew more intense, his singing grew louder. As her tears plunged harder, his dancing spun faster. It was all one, long, painful blur.

Finally, Laurie's body gave out completely and collapsed to the floor. Royce's ghost evaporated, and the room fell silent. There had been no battle. There hadn't even been a skirmish. She was disgusted with herself for not being stronger; for not having the willpower to throw a single punch. It seemed that even the thought of fighting God was enough to defeat her.

She lay stagnant with one side of her face buried in the carpet. She was, and had been for so long, completely exhausted—mentally, emotionally, and spiritually. All energy had been siphoned from her body and her mind. Tears left the corner of her eyes and trickled down the side of her face, creating a puddle in her ear. Her eyes fluttered open and closed. Her breaths slowed down to long, heavy sighs—the kind of sighs that settle on your chest right before you enter into a deep slumber that lasts for hours.

Laurie's eyes shot open.

Something under Royce's bed caught her attention. She wiped away tears to clear her vision and propped herself up on one elbow. She began to reach under his bed but snapped her arm back suddenly, as if scared by a spider. She shouldn't do this. Even though Royce was gone, it still felt like snooping. When he was alive, she had made it a point to give him space, to not make him feel suffocated like other parents did when they hovered over their kids. In the end, it was her own selfishness that had created an even greater space between them. Now, she had to live with the knowledge that the space she had created had contributed to his death.

Laurie shook the thoughts away. No, she had done enough damage. What more could she possibly do? She had to know what the object was. Reaching in slowly, she pulled out a brown leather book. Its edges were tattered, and a thin layer of dust blanketed the front cover. Outlining its border was what looked like Celtic symbols of swords, shields, and armor. A thin strap of leather encompassed the book to keep it shut, held together by a smooth wooden clasp. Laurie had never seen this book before, but then again, she hadn't paid much attention to any of Royce's possessions in the last few months. A quick stab of pain jolted through her. She winced it away.

Removing the wooden clasp from the leather strap, she gently opened the book. Like a miniature sun rising, the book cover rose from its pages and lay flat on the floor. Two words were stamped across the inside cover:

Royce's Journal

Laurie's face grew pale. She had no idea that Royce had kept a journal or that he was even into journaling. Had she really been that oblivious? Was it sketches, notes to a girl that he liked, or dreams of what he wanted to be when he grew up? Were the pages filled with hope and healing or disgrace and despair? He had seen so much, *too* much. He rarely shared his thoughts with her because she had closed herself off from listening to him. Now, there was so much that she wanted to know about her little boy. It grieved her to think that she would have to read about those things through a diary rather than having conversations sitting on the front porch eating ice cream together.

Her hands shivered as she turned to the first page. The creases moaned in disapproval after not being opened in months. Another spasm of pain shot through Laurie. It had been *months* since she had heard his voice. She swallowed hard and smoothed out the page. At the top, a title was written in smudged ink:

August 18, 2016: What to Do When
the Clouds Grow Dark

She snapped the book shut, terrified at the words she might read and the guilt she might feel. Whatever his thoughts were, they were just that, *his* thoughts. They weren't someone else's opinion about how he *might* feel. They were her son's deepest secrets. Maybe what intimidated Laurie the most was actually hearing from Royce again. She knew that he would be forgiving, that he was kind and compassionate and loyal. But still, could she bear it?

After sitting for what seemed like hours, long after the sun had gone down and stars glittered the sky, Laurie decided to read the journal. In the end, her decision had really come down to one basic thought: the fear of never knowing her son more intimately outweighed the fear of facing his memory. It was this intimate longing that drove the book open again, and it was with this great fear that she began to read.

> A few days ago, I was walking home from school. The sun had left, the rain had come, and my Spider-Man backpack was getting soaked. But I danced in the puddles and sang to the sky because that's what you do when the clouds grow dark. I used to think that all people did that when the clouds got dark, but I am beginning to realize that some people see the sky a little different than other people.

For the next three hours, Laurie sat helplessly in the middle of Royce's bedroom. She read and reread paragraphs over and over again. She didn't eat, she didn't drink, and she never took her eyes off of the pages. At times, she even had to remind herself to breathe. To say it was overwhelming would have been to rob it of its true impact. Laurie was transfixed, horrified, awestruck. Each word that she read drove a stake deeper into her soul, whether out of gratefulness or regret. She wept periodically and held the book close to her chest, clutching it as if she could somehow squeeze Royce out of its pages.

By the time she got to her son's last written words, her eyes throbbed and her throat ached from the tears that had refused to quit interrupting her. She read the last paragraph in stunned silence, paralyzed by the finality in the words.

> If the feeling is true, then I don't know how much time I'll have to write anymore. That may sound a little crazy, but sometimes we just know that something is going to happen. Not because someone tells us, or because we were given a sign, but because we just know. And all we can do when it does happen is try to be brave and remember who we are in that moment. So if my feeling is right and something does happen, then know that it has been a pleasure getting to share my story with you.

The journal slid out of Laurie's hands, not because she had dropped it, but because her fingers couldn't grasp what she had just read. Royce hadn't just been the victim of a crime. He had been the victim of freedom. He had been the victim of truth. He had been the victim of *redemption*. Royce had reached out to those who some considered untouchable. He had given a voice to those who could not find their own. He had accepted everyone, not because of their skin color or their religion, but because everyone deserved to be loved. What a precious soul her boy had been, far beyond anything she had ever recognized.

Somehow, his ten-year-old mind had been able to grasp that there is a distinct difference between what we say and who we are. That we don't get remembered for what we intend to do but for what our lives produce. That the only way to *produce* anything of substance was to *be* a person of substance. She understood that clearly now. Maybe the greatest tragedy in the world is not fear or loneliness or pride, but a counterfeit heart refusing to love. Words are only as good as the actions that support them; actions are only as good as the motives that drive them; motives are only as good as the love that births them. And Royce's love had been authentic.

So many things made sense: things he had alluded to, people he had referenced, days that he had gone straight to his room when getting home from school, random bruises he claimed happened on the playground. The stories he had written about meshed with the reality she had experienced. It all finally made sense. And she had been too selfish to help change any of it. She was completely and totally lost, hypnotized by guilt and shame.

Her son was a far better person than she had been, or ever would be. He deserved life. She was the one who deserved death. But life had chosen her and left him to face the shadows alone.

The full weight of Royce's words compounded together. It *was* more than she could bear. Laurie's body convulsed as she slumped over and began hyperventilating. For the next few moments, the room was silent except for her deep gasps and shuddering cries. She fought to fill her lungs with air, again and again and again.

Royce.

Her baby boy.

Taken away.

Ripped away.

Her joy.

Her hero.

Her *fault*.

She focused on the comic book rug beneath her, trying to redirect her mind and gain control of her body. Air crept back into her lungs, a smidgen at a time. But even after she began breathing semi-normally, she fought to breathe deeper, as if trying to conserve as much air as she could before it ran out of supply.

Laurie turned her head and caught another glimpse of the picture on the nightstand—innocent, unharmed, wholesome. The picture was the peace before the storm—a storm that she had allowed to destroy her life, and thus, destroy his life. It was here in front of her, in the pages he had written. The words would forever be tattooed on her soul. They were the smoldering ashes of what was and the smoke residue of what could have been. And she had let the fire burn out.

In that moment, she knew what had to be done. The picture had told her. Royce's smile had told her. Royce's journal had told her. Her ghosts had told her. Above all, the battle that wasn't a battle, had told her. She wasn't surprised because that's what happens when people attempt to pray—things change. Now was her chance to finally do something about it.

Her heart still beating fast, Laurie grabbed Royce's journal and crawled on her hands and knees across the floor toward the doorway to her bedroom.

Chapter 8
What Had to Be Done

Laurie grappled with the doorframe to help pull herself up. Her legs were asleep from lying on them for the past few hours, which made it difficult at first to move across the room. She was still breathing hard, though stable finally. Sliding one hand along the wall for balance, she made her way to her dresser.

She slid open the top drawer and dug through crusty socks that had been poorly washed. An odor drifted into the air, but she took little notice of it. There were far more important things happening. Once she found what she was looking for, she slid the drawer halfway closed, too careless to close it completely. Soon, it wouldn't matter anyway. She walked the remaining few feet over to her bed and eased into it.

Rain had begun to fall outside, the droplets creating a hypnotic pattern against the window. The sound helped soothe her fragile nerves. She was tempted to let sleep overtake her and drift away until morning. Then, she could finish what she had started. Maybe a little rest and a fresh whiskey in the morning would help encourage . . .

Thunder clashed, like a judge hammering his gavel. It ended any debate that was surfacing in her mind. Even the thunder knew that the time was now and that there was no room for excuses. Laurie reached down and pulled out a half empty liter of Coke that was sticking out from under the bed. She had no clue how long it had been there, but once again, there were more important things happening. It would do the job, and that's all that mattered. She had to remain focused.

Glancing down, her eyes rested on the objects in her hands. One hand held the bottle of Coke. The other hand clutched a bottle of OxyContin. She rotated the orange, plastic container and watched the white pills tumble over each other. Eerie moonlight shone through the water-strewn window, casting shadows of raindrops around the prescription label. The spots looked like tribal villagers dancing at a sacrificial bonfire.

She had seen movies where people had contemplated suicide, and each scene was decorated with flashbacks from their past, memories that had been lost, words that were left unspoken, and regrets in every shape and form. She often wondered what thoughts would plague her mind in her last moments on earth. Now, she knew. It was an image of her finger tracing the outline of the words on her son's grave. That is the only image that she cared about. It was a culmination of everything that had ever gone wrong in her life. That image symbolized everything she was and everything she wasn't; everything she had lived for and everything she couldn't live without. This wasn't a movie, and nothing had prepared her for the terror that seized her. Yet she continued because that was all that was left to do.

The Coke bottle was silent as she unscrewed the lid, but the pill bottle screamed relentlessly as its top was removed. She poured a few pills onto the sheets beside her and brushed them into a neat pile. After a few seconds, she thought better of it and emptied the entire bottle. She didn't want to come back from wherever she was going. She just wanted the pain to be over. A single tear landed next to the pile of pills, creating a tiny wet circle in the bed sheet.

She carefully counted out five pills and scooped them up. She raised her hand to her mouth and paused. Was this real? Was she doing the right thing? A picture from her own nightstand called out to her. It displayed Royce and his father, the Christmas before he had left them. They were making Christmas tree cookies together, putting red icing on the tips of the branches. Royce had icing smeared across his cheek, and Laurie's head was tilted back laughing. A moment of pure joy.

A flash of lightning illuminated the room, making her jump. It was the courtroom finding her guilty, sentencing her to a life of damnation. The two loves of her life were waiting for her. Her decision was final.

She dropped the pills onto her tongue, lifted the Coke bottle, and swallowed.

Her first step to a new life.

Rain pelted the window harder, as if offering her its affirmation. Royce stared in through the window at Laurie. His expressionless face hung in the shadows, his hands pressed against the glass. His breath lightly fogged the window as he inhaled and exhaled. A shot of lightening lit the frame, and his face disappeared. Laurie picked up a few more pills and washed them down smoothly.

She snuggled deeper into the sheets, pulling the comforter over her body. It would be her final resting place. There was no need to write a note or leave something behind. Anyone who knew her well enough knew that she had lived a tortured life, so her death would be self-explanatory. She was bitter at no one other than the person she had planned to meet soon. The one she had lost the battle to. The one who had a lot of explaining to do. Finally, she would get to look him in the face and tell him how he had abandoned her and forgotten her and left her depleted. It was her turn to see the pain in his eyes.

Laurie began to pick up one pill at a time, savoring each last drop of life. Oddly, she didn't feel scared, but sad. Sad that things had to be this way. Sad that she couldn't have made things better. Sad that she couldn't live life without her husband and her son—the two greatest things that had ever happened to her. This propelled her further, the motion of her arm rising to her mouth becoming mechanical. The pile that seemed to never end was slowly growing smaller, as was her world.

The room began to swoon. Thunder that was once monstrous and overpowering had now wilted away into a dull roar. Lightning that had quickly flashed across her room now illuminated the walls for seconds at a time. Raindrops trudged down her window like thick honey. Everything grew slower. Sounds muted, and lights faded in and out. The world's engine was shutting down, its gears making their final rotations.

Laurie heard crying that wasn't her own, but when her head lolled around, all she saw were clothes littering the floor and walls that stood bare. They all shook as if an earthquake was hitting her apartment.

She swallowed another pill.

Hopelessness and surrender fought through her veins, both claiming the territory.

She started to lose her balance and slump sideways, but she forced herself to stay upright. She couldn't stop now. She had lost so many battles in her life, but this was one battle she would win. She had come too far to fail. She would finish what she started.

With one final surge of energy, she emptied as many pills as she could into her mouth and gulped them down. Her last thoughts were of the burn in her throat, the chill on her skin, and the smile of a "would have been eleven-year-old" boy. The room turned black as the world stopped completely.

Laurie's head sagged to her pillow.

The engines turned off.

Her eyes went still.

The rain stopped and the thunder quit rolling and all of nature watched as one of its own faded down a dark, lonely tunnel.

Chapter 9
The World of White

Laurie opened her eyes.

Above her, the world had completely disappeared, as if its colors had been erased and left barren. Without moving her head, she rolled her eyes in every direction to try and grasp her surroundings—up, down, left, right, and up again. Nothing but a canvas of white sky stretched to all corners of her vision. Even though she had no rational way to support the thought, she was seized with a sense of how small she was in comparison to the place she had awoken to.

Confusion and doubt closed their hands around her neck, cutting off her air and making her throat feel like it was swelling. Her body went rigid, engulfed by the bare world that seemed to swallow her whole. What was she doing here? And what was *here*?

She hadn't really known what to expect when taking her own life, but she for sure hadn't expected to be so alert or aware or even . . . *awake*. She was too conscious of the emptiness around her, which worried her even more. Had she tried to escape life only to live again? Had she gone from one tortured life to another? She stared hopelessly into the nothingness while the nothingness stared hopelessly back.

She clenched her fingers into a fist, scraping the edges of the ground . . .

Wait.

She tilted her head to the side and turned her hand over. As her fingers bloomed open, she saw a small white pile of substance in the middle of her palm. It looked like she had dipped her hand in powdered sugar. She formed a fist again, feeling the substance harden within her grasp and pack together in a tight ball. She opened her hand slowly. The shape of her fingers was left imprinted in the pebble-looking object. Was that . . . *snow*?

Laurie sat up. Before she could marvel at her new environment, her own body captured her intrigue. The grimy clothes she had been wearing when she collapsed into bed had been replaced with a white dress that stretched to her ankles. It was elegant, not from its design but because it was untainted. It had an aura of cleanliness that Laurie had never seen before. Never *felt* before. She grasped it, feeling its texture and wondering if any of it was real.

Sinking her hands into the snow, Laurie shoved off the ground and stood to her feet. She brought her hands together to wipe them off, but they were completely dry. Her eyebrows furrowed in confusion. She looked at her open hands again, but no hint of moisture could be found on them. Laurie looked down cautiously. There was no imprint of her body either. But it was snow. She was sure of it. So how could there not be any trace of her lying on the ground?

Her gaze lifted from her feet, to the ground in front of her, to the land in the distance. A quiet gasp leapt from her mouth. Rolling hills of white snow stretched as far as she could see, expanding further and further until they faded into the horizon. There, a hazy mist blended the hills and sky together, making it difficult to see where one ended and the other began.

The hills were, quite literally, perfect. There were no patches of green earth breaking through the surface, no fallen logs peppering an otherwise pure landscape, and no tracks from a road or path winding their way across the plains. Nothing. It looked like someone had taken a universe-sized, spotless blanket and laid it across the earth.

Laurie turned in circles, surveying everything around her. More snow. More hills. More white surfaces. The terrain was so bright that she had to squint to prevent her eyes from hurting. If she had felt small before, she felt miniscule now. She was a tiny imperfection contaminating the vast hemisphere.

Imperfection. Imperfect. *Dead.*

She was dead.

So this is what it felt like? She had heard of countless people theorizing about the afterlife. Theories of heaven and hell, eternal damnation, ultimate perfection, expansions of time, other realities, universes flowing with reward. She wondered how many others had traveled before her, expecting streets of gold, or lakes of fire, or pleasure, or torture, and had instead, arrived at this: desolation. Which perhaps bothered her even more. If millions had gone before her, then where was everyone? She appeared to be the only one in this world, if that's what it was.

A hint of movement snapped Laurie to attention. To her left, rose the highest arching hill in her immediate vicinity. The summit was just high enough to hide what lay behind it, like a cliff ledge that led to a great beyond. It was beautiful, yet intimidating. And it was there, at the top of the hill with nothing but the sky as a curtain behind it, that something had shifted.

Laurie squinted her eyes further in nervous concentration. A figure began to emerge at the crest of the hill. Little by little, it came into view; first its head, then its neck, and finally its full body.

Standing motionless, firm in place, was a massive, white horse.

It was perhaps the most magnificent animal that Laurie had ever seen in person. She had grown up around horses in the South her entire life, yet this one captivated her in a way that she couldn't describe. The second it appeared on the hilltop horizon, she felt connected to it. The horse focused on her, as if it knew that she had arrived and had come to find her; as if its presence there was intentional and therefore *her* presence was intentional. She stood entranced, not knowing what to do but feeling that it was okay.

The horse seemed to answer Laurie's subconscious curiosity and began trotting down the snowy embankment. Its coat shimmered amidst the solid white backdrop, like rays of sunlight reflecting off of the face of a watch. The horse's hooves glided effortlessly in the snow, giving it an appearance of a ghost floating across the surface. What was even more peculiar was that the horse left no tracks in its wake. The second that each hoof lifted, the snow fell back into place, leaving no trace that any traveler had passed through it.

It reached the bottom of the hill and drew nearer to Laurie, slowing its pace as it approached her. The horse was every bit magnificent up close as it had been in the distance. Muscles rippled from its hind legs, shoulders, and chest. Its mane lay calmly against one side of its neck, luscious and full. The hair around its hooves was also white, making it appear that all four legs had sprouted from the earth—a statue carved out of a block of snow and ice.

The only features distinguishable from the rest of its body were the insides of its ears and nostrils, which were colored a dark charcoal. The way that they defied the rest of horse made them even more dynamic.

And the horse's eyes.

Glossy black.

Swirling with life. And death.

They locked onto Laurie, disabling her from looking anywhere else. The eyes searched the innermost parts of her being—the heart of her soul. They knew her. She could feel it. They knew the person she was and the person she was not. They knew what she had done and what she had left undone. They knew her mistakes, her faults, her failures. And they didn't look away.

Laurie had an overwhelming urge to know those eyes. She wanted to hear them share their thoughts and emotions and desires. She wanted them to tell her what dark secrets they held and what she was doing in this place.

But they simply stared, patient, unwavering.

Purposeful.

Laurie couldn't quite grasp the reality of what was happening, but as she peered into its eyes, into their deep sea of darkness, she knew something as well. They held the key to everything—the answers that she had been looking for. So as the horse turned, and its presence alone beckoned her to follow, she didn't hesitate.

It trotted back in the direction it had come, its mane lightly bouncing against its neck with each gallop.

Out of instinct, Laurie picked up the edges of her dress so that she wouldn't trip on them. That's when she saw that her feet were bare. *Bare but not cold*, she mused. The tan color of her toes looked out of place against the innocent ground beneath them. She scrunched her feet together, collecting the snow between her toes and watching it clump together. It was a strange feeling to stand in snow and not be freezing. Her feet were not warm, but maybe . . . cozy?

She felt a shadow pass over her, even though the light had not changed, and she looked up. The horse had stopped walking. It was staring over its shoulder at her, as if scorning her for not focusing on the mission at hand. Laurie felt a quick jolt of anxiety, sensing that this was something that she could not mess up. She needed to see where this horse was leading her.

She started moving, and the horse resumed its journey up the high mound in front of them. Laurie walked faster, not wanting to lose pace with it again. Trudging through the snow almost made her feel guilty, as if she was corrupting it, as if her steps didn't belong. But she had no other choice. Surely, she was not the first to invade its territory.

The bank inclined further as they began their ascent to the top of the hill. The surface of the snow had looked very deep, but with each step, Laurie found that it barely rose to her ankle bone. She looked behind her, and just like the horse, no tracks were visible. Maybe this was a sign that she belonged after all? Each time her foot lifted, the snow fell perfectly back into its place. She wanted to observe the phenomenon more, but it slowed her down. She forced herself to look straight ahead.

Climbing the hill reminded her of her childhood. On rare occasions, her parents allowed her to go to a nearby theme park with her friends. Their favorite roller coaster had a huge incline that seemed to take forever to climb. As their car clinked and shuddered its way up the rails, their anticipation grew more intense. They always stared at the blue sky in front of them and gripped their handlebars tighter as they approached the summit. Even though they knew what lay on the other side, the suspense was always there, waiting to explode.

As Laurie looked to the top of the hill, that same nervous anticipation rose inside of her. She was slowly shuddering and clinking higher, aware that after a brief pause at the top, she would plunge forward into whatever fate awaited her. The difference now was that she didn't know what was on the other side. This wasn't a theme park. This was death.

The horse reached the peak first and stationed itself in place, patiently waiting for Laurie to finish the journey to the top. Moments later, Laurie joined it, breathing deep and quivering lightly, despite the fact that her body wasn't cold.

She looked back down the hill from where she had begun the climb. The view was overwhelming. The white world was just as spotless, just as clear, but even more breathtaking. It was amazing how even a slight change in elevation could completely alter the image of a landscape. Of course, there was no sign of where she had woken on the ground, but she knew it was there somewhere.

The horse's body flickered in her peripheral vision, signaling Laurie that it was time to move on. Laurie turned to follow the horse, which had already begun its descent.

She stopped abruptly.

The slope dipped into a quaint valley that lay below them. In the middle of the flat arena was a small lake with a single weeping willow stationed beside it. Its long branches hung daintily from its body, the snow outlining each arm. She had loved those trees since she was a little girl. The whole setting was serene. Both the lake and the tree looked at rest.

But it wasn't the lake or the willow that had piqued her interest. Her eyes were drawn to the hill behind them where an enormous, white barn sat in waiting. It was difficult to see against the backdrop of everything white, but there was no mistaking it. Its broad presence, resting on the hill, was confident and secure. And like the horse, Laurie felt lured toward it, compelled to discover the mysteries that lay within it.

In front of her, the horse had nearly reached the willow. Laurie picked up her pace and started jogging, careful to not trip down the embankment. It soon leveled out, which allowed her to move quicker.

As she passed the lake, she marveled at its uniqueness. There was no wind, no ripples, and no waves lapping onto shore. It was still. In fact, *too* still. If it had not been for the reflection of the willow on the surface of the water, she might not have known the lake was even there. The territory around it and the sky above it were so bright that their reflection on the lake made the lake itself almost invisible. She had a sudden urge to launch into the water and disrupt its peaceful meditation, but the awareness of the barn propelled her forward.

The hill that approached the barn was not as steep as the first one they had mounted, but the incline extended further into the distance, making the hike seem more tiresome. The closer they came to the barn, the more Laurie's mind filled with questions. Why was it there? Did anyone live there? Was it the only sign of life in this world? Why was the horse taking her there?

Too many questions and not enough answers. It had become the pattern of Laurie's life. Well, her old life, at least. She tried to dismiss the thoughts and worked to catch up to the horse.

Together, they continued their trek toward the lonesome barn.

She glanced behind her again. The lake and the tree had grown smaller, though remained unchanged. Laurie didn't know why she kept looking back. Maybe to make sure that the world wasn't being wiped away like her footprints? Then again, what would it matter?

This was her afterlife.

The horse began to stir, snapping Laurie's head back around. The barn loomed ahead. The horse began digging at the snow with its hooves, its tail flicking and its head biting. It looked like it was wrestling with itself to contain the energy that was waiting to unleash. The horse whinnied loudly, a high-pitched squeal that sputtered off into soft nickers. It was the first time that Laurie had heard the horse make any noise. What was it about the presence of the barn that had ignited its spirit?

Without warning, the horse started galloping toward the barn doors. It sprinted faster than it had before, no longer looking to see if Laurie was following. Its hooves slung snow in the air as its mane streamed behind it. If Laurie wasn't so caught off guard, she might have marveled at how elegant the horse looked running through the snow. It truly was majestic.

The horse stopped abruptly at the doors, stamping its feet and flicking its head back and forth. Laurie finally reached the doors as well, out of breath and bewildered. She had been so focused on keeping up with the horse that she hadn't even thought about the anxiety of approaching the barn.

Now that she could calm her breathing, she looked up at the structure in front of her. It was painted white like the snow, made completely of wood, and had gambrel roofing. There were open-aired stalls on both sides of the barn with slated roofs covering them. In the center of the entrance stood two enormous doors that closed in the middle. Snow outlined each edge of the barn. It was so defined that it looked like the snow had been painted there rather than fallen into place.

Laurie gaped at the barn, amazed at its size and construction. The wonder of it only brought her back to the question that had entered her mind the moment she saw it: what was a barn like this doing in a world like this? In a lifeless world where hopeless souls like herself came to be damned?

She assumed that the doors would either open on their own or that the horse would lead her inside, but neither happened. Instead, the horse quit making noises and stood completely still. It looked solemn, the way it had looked when Laurie first saw it appear at the top of the hill. Its eyes pierced the air, and its hooves stood firmly planted in the ground.

It stared at her.

Stared *past* her.

Laurie followed its gaze. Her breath caught in her throat. Her heart pounded in her ears. Her limbs went numb. She collapsed to her knees, easing into the snow as if reverently bowing before a prince.

Hiking up the other side of the hill was her eleven-year-old son.

Chapter 10
Reunited

For the first time in a very long time, her vision wasn't seeing double or shifting or blacking out. She was seeing clearly— clearer than she might have ever seen before. It was him. It was her boy.

Unlike herself, he was dressed to survive a blizzard. He had on a wool hat that fit snuggly over his ears and insulated gloves that made his hands look enlarged. He wore a thick parka with fur lining the hood. His baggy snowboarding pants surrounded his boots, which kicked up heavy piles of snow each time one of them stepped forward. He was so bundled up that he could have been mistaken by anyone for anyone. But Laurie knew it was him.

She knew it from the way his shoulders bounced up and down when he walked, from the way his arms swung limply back and forth like a stringed puppet, from the way his head shifted side to side, just like it did every time he danced in rhythm to the song he was singing. She knew it was him because their hearts were still intertwined, and the heart knows when it has found its source of pleasure.

Laurie watched him in disbelief as the distance between them grew smaller. Her face grew hot, and her forehead began to sweat. Her heartbeat was so loud that it seemed to drown out every other noise but her own labored breathing. She tried to swallow, but her throat was too dry. Every conscious feeling in her body eroded away.

She knew that he was really there, yet she didn't know how to believe it. How to grasp it. How it could be real.

In this world, he was *alive.*

In her daydreams, Laurie had tried to envision what it would be like to see her son again. She had played scenario after scenario but could never settle on a particular image. Partly because she had no idea how he would react. Would he be angry, sad, forgiving? And how would she react to his reaction? Would she cry, smile, sink into her own regret? Often, the thought of it was too overwhelming, so she forced her mind to retreat elsewhere.

But now that he was here, right in front of her, she was forced to face those feelings. She could no longer retreat. No scenario had prepared her for this, and no emotion seemed to grasp what her heart was aching. At the core of her wondering, she knew that when the time came, *if* the time came, she would not know what to do. And she didn't. She was completely lost. All she could do was sit helplessly on her knees and attempt to capture the reality that was being created with each second.

When Royce was just a few yards away, he stopped walking. The wool from his hood partly covered his face, but Laurie could still see his blue eyes shimmering beneath it. They splintered every fiber of her being and froze the blood running through her veins. She held her breath, waiting . . .

Royce looked into her eyes, his gaze paralyzing. Then, a large grin broke out across his face. It was a grin that she knew all too well, a grin that mended her heart and tore it into further pieces at the same time.

"Hi, Mother," Royce said and held out his arms.

Tears wet her cheeks, cool and soothing against her skin.

Laurie couldn't move. The snow beneath her turned to glue, holding her firm in place. She opened her mouth to speak but only found quivering lips trying to form words.

Her gaze finally broke, and her chin drooped to her chest. Tears fell silently into the snow, disappearing the second they landed. Laurie took two deep breaths and looked up at Royce again, who was now kneeling in front of her. Before she could react, he engulfed her body, wrapping his arms around her and pulling her into his chest.

Hesitantly, she folded her arms around him as well, basking in the surreal feeling of being close to her son again.

Except that it was not her son.

Not the Royce she had known, at least. Not the boy who loved his Spider-Man backpack and *Power Rangers* action figures. Not the boy who sang to the sky and played in the rain and took care of her when she was sick. Not him.

Even through the thick jacket that he wore, Laurie could feel a strange energy circulating throughout his body. It was like his body was not made of bones and muscle and skin, but of a constant flow of electricity that never slowed down. It was warm, vibrant. As she hugged him, the energy seemed to flood from his body into her own, making her feel more alert and awake. He looked like the same boy she had said goodbye to months before, but she knew that boy no longer existed.

Royce released her, still beaming with a wide smile. She tried to smile in return but could only offer a look of astonishment.

"My baby boy . . . is it . . . is it really you?" She grazed his cheek with her fingertips. Short bursts of electricity omitted from his skin, shooting tingling waves through her hand.

"Of course, Mother, but not exactly as you remember me. It is impossible to stay the same once you arrive in this place." He spoke matter-of-factly, with a confidence that was both mature and graceful.

"But what is this place?" Laurie asked timidly.

Royce's smile never wavered. "This is a place where we can see things . . . things that we could not have seen in any other way."

"I don't understand. How are you here? Is this . . . *heaven?*" Laurie looked around again, as if expecting to see something different than she had seen before.

Royce stood up and helped Laurie to her feet. Then, he slipped off both gloves and stuffed them gently into his jacket pocket. "No, this is not heaven, although it *is* absolutely gorgeous." He looked out over the valley at the tranquil lake and the single weeping willow that accompanied it, then scanned the seemingly endless mounds of snowy hilltops. He gazed at the world as if he was seeing it all for the first time. Laurie couldn't help but marvel at the way he looked entranced, stricken by the world's beauty. In that moment, he was the Royce she had always known: curious, intrigued, mystified at his surroundings. The clarity of the world reflected in his eyes, accentuating their baby blue hue. He smiled to himself, his eyes still captivated by the landscape. "Not heaven, but closely linked. He wanted me to bring you here."

"Who is, *he*?" Laurie asked. But she already knew.

Royce offered her a sympathetic smile, as if he was aware of her understanding, and after a brief pause, he continued, "I know that He isn't the person you want to hear about right now. He understands that. But He also understands that the thing we deny the most is often where the root of healing must begin."

Laurie looked down at her naked feet. Her toes fidgeted in the snow just as they had fidgeted in the gravel of their church parking lot when she was talking to Pastor Scoggins. Her cheeks were growing warm again, but not from shock. It was a mixture of confusion, irritation, and hurt all rising to the surface. Royce was right, she knew it, but that didn't stop her bitter feelings from bubbling over. Any discussion about *Him* was a quick trigger that she struggled to keep under control.

Royce placed a comforting hand on her shoulder and leaned in close, as if to whisper to her. "He knows that the hurt is very deep, Mother. He knows it because when your heart wrenches in pain, His spirit cries out with you. He feels what you feel. I know that doesn't make any sense to you, and I know that you are flooded with more questions than you can handle, but that's why He allowed me to bring you here. He knows that our healing doesn't come from the questions we get answered but from the peace we choose to find. This world is meant to help you discover that peace."

With her head still bowed in defeat and tears muddling her words, Laurie whispered in return, "There is no peace for me, Royce. Not anymore. That's why I'm here, in this place. Because the pain was greater than the peace, and every string of hope inside of me broke."

Royce took both of her wrists in his hands and gave them a reassuring squeeze.

"The reason you are here, Mother, is because He isn't finished with you yet."

Laurie shook her head, still in disbelief. She didn't know what to think of Royce's words. Seeing her son alone would have been fine, but at the mention of *Him*, the dam of her heart had already begun to shut out any water that tried to surge through and hydrate her spirit. Plus, even if she was willing to be healed, she didn't know where she would begin.

All she could do was stand in silence, unsure of what to say and how to say it. But once again, Royce appeared to have heard the dialogue of her inner thoughts.

"He doesn't expect you to know all the answers—what to think, how to make sense of everything, how to find temporary relief to a permanent tragedy. He doesn't expect anyone to figure those things out on their own . . . and that is why I am here. That is why you are here. For me to show you."

"Show me what?" Laurie asked. So far, the world they inhabited was void of all life. She didn't know what Royce could possibly hope to show her in this environment.

"Show you what you could not see on your own . . . what you *chose* not to see on your own."

"I don't know what else there is to see," Laurie responded quickly. "The problem isn't that I can't see. The problem is that I have seen too much." She was trying to maintain her composure, but already she was growing frustrated at the conversation.

Royce spoke in a calm manner, as if he were reinforcing a lesson to his own son. "There is a difference between seeing and having vision, Mother. You have only seen what you have chosen to see within the parameters of your pain. The life He wants you to pursue is beyond the boundaries you have created for yourself. We must tear down those borders. Only then can you hope to heal, and only *then* can you hope to change. Let Him exchange your limited sight for His *limitless* vision."

Laurie wanted to agree, wanted to believe her son, but her emotions kept blinding her. For so long, her pain was all she had to comfort her. It was consistent, reliable. Letting it go would be like erasing part of herself. She wanted to forget about the pain, but at the same time, she was terrified to release it. "I'm sorry, Royce . . . I . . . well, I did what I did because the journey could finally end. I needed it to end. And now, you're telling me that it isn't over? That I have to be forced to understand it? No, that's not fair. Why can't He allow the pain to win? I don't understand . . ."

Royce acknowledged her words and drew her to himself. "He has not called you to understand, but He *has* called you to believe. Please, Mother, for my sake, and for the sake of so many others that you aren't even aware of yet, will you allow me to show you?"

Laurie had already exhausted every bit of emotion that she had possessed in her previous life. She wasn't even sure if she was alive now, and the last thing she wanted was to reopen old wounds. But Royce's words latched onto her like a disease.

Please, Mother, for my sake . . .

She couldn't bear to see anymore disappointment in her son's eyes. She didn't know how it would change anything, but she owed it to him to at least follow through with what he was asking her to do. "Okay, Royce . . . okay, my precious boy. How will you show me?"

Laurie thought that he would be overjoyed, grateful for her willingness to follow him. Instead, his expression grew serious, and his tone lowered. "Since there is an infinite number of factors that contribute to pain in people's lives, everyone's journey to healing is uniquely different. Some people will need to focus on particular areas of healing that others will not. There is no singular 'fix all' solution. So this will be your journey and yours alone."

"Okay," Laurie said, grasping the concept but still unable to grasp the overall purpose of why she had arrived in the new world.

"To understand what to fix, we must find where you are hurt, and to find where you are hurt, we must locate the root of the suffering. This won't be easy, Mother. Healing never is. But it's not about what is easy. It's about what is necessary. If we do not explore our pain, then we will never build up the endurance we need to heal from it."

Royce took his mother's hand and gripped it tightly in his own. She half-expected some type of transportation to appear that would take them on this journey—a vehicle, or a sleigh, or even the white horse. Wait, where was the white horse? She was so caught up in seeing Royce again that she had completely forgotten about it. She glanced around quickly, but it was nowhere in sight. A tug on her arm reminded her that there were more important matters at hand. Laurie let Royce guide her, mentally preparing for a long trek through the snow. Instead, he turned her around and led her to the entrance of the barn.

The doors loomed before them, gigantic and menacing. Laurie thought the barn had looked so innocent when she had seen it as just a barn. She had fooled herself in thinking that the horse had brought her here just to meet Royce. Now, she was filled with new trepidation. The barn held everything behind its doors: her fears, her failures, her doubts, her demons. It was amazing that a breathtaking place could instill such terror.

Royce paused in front of the entrance and turned to Laurie one last time. "Just know, Mother, that your pain was never wasted. He drew significance from it. He orchestrated His purpose within it. The heartache *will* lead to healing, and I'll be with you every step of the journey."

He reached for the door.

Chapter 11
Amidst the Flames

Royce strategically positioned one hand on each door and steadily began sliding them apart. Laurie watched him, lost in thought. Years ago, Royce had brought home a storybook that he had won at Vacation Bible School. He had excitedly flipped to the story of Samson (one of his favorites), where a picture revealed a man pushing apart stone pillars in front of a crowd of people. Laurie knew that the story ended with the pillars collapsing and thousands of people dying, including Samson. As she observed her son exerting his strength with his arms outstretched, she couldn't help but wonder if the sight of him in that same position foreshadowed her own death inside the barn. An icy chill swept down her spine. She thought that she was already dead, yet she felt a foreboding sense that her pain wasn't finished.

Laurie shook off the notion and turned her attention back to Royce, who had since let go of the doors. He stepped back and kindly bowed his hand before his mother, bidding her to enter first. She walked through the entrance, passing from a world of light into a world of shadows.

The open doors behind Laurie offered just enough light to illuminate the features inside the barn. She stood before a massive rectangular room whose solid white interior was all but bare. On either side of her, balconies supported by colossal beams spanned the length of the barn. At their far ends, narrow staircases descended diagonally to meet at a landing in the middle, which dumped out onto the ground floor. Under the balconies, closed square windows lined the walls that opened to the stalls outside. Towering above her, arched wooden beams crisscrossed higher and higher until they meshed together at the peak of the ceiling.

Laurie had been aware of the size of the barn when she was outside, but now that she was inside, the vastness of the room consumed her in an entirely new way. She nervously cleared her throat, knowing that it was too late to turn back (and that she had nowhere to go even if she wanted to turn back). She had chosen this fate.

As Royce closed the barn doors, the outside world faded, leaving them in a blanket of darkness. It was then that Laurie noticed what she could have sworn hadn't been there before—a small campfire burning in the middle of the room.

There was nothing to prevent it from spreading, yet it remained corralled in a neat circle. Laurie was overcome by a strange conviction. Its presence somehow conveyed that, while it contained the power to engulf the entire universe, it chose to keep itself here, in this space, composed and restrained. No one held any power over it, for it could not be created or destroyed. Laurie suddenly felt as if she had completely lost control. She had always grasped her pain tightly, careful to not let anyone pry it from her hands. But now, it wasn't hers anymore. Not here. Not in the presence of the fire.

Her eyes fixated on the flames. The first thing that struck her as odd was that there was no wood to keep the fire burning. The flames slithered out of the ground cackling and hissing with no apparent source of power. Laurie had never witnessed a fire without some type of energy to fuel it. And perhaps stranger than the lack of wood was the lack of color.

The flames were white.

Not golden, or yellow, or even a misty grey. They were white, like the snow outside and the wood of the barn and the horse that had led her here. They were transparent yet solid, their tongues in a constant state of flux.

"Amazing, isn't it?"

Laurie flinched, letting out a soft cry. She had momentarily forgotten about Royce. He stood beside her, his hands behind his back and his eyes focused on the fire. Laurie saw the reflection of the scene in his eyes, the light of the flames contrasting with the dark complexion of his face inside the barn. She thought that he would continue talking, but he seemed content to bask in the silence. She didn't know what to do, so she stood beside him and stared at the fire as well.

The flames rose and fell, biting at the air and evaporating into the atmosphere. Laurie was fascinated by the way they highlighted certain aspects of the barn. Like how the flames cast a soft glow on the white beams that held up the balconies, making them appear like ghost soldiers standing at attention. Or how the fire made the arches of the ceiling zigzag with shadows, transforming them into gigantic spider webs. Royce was right, it was amazing.

Besides the fire, the only other source of light came from the cracks in the wooden slats of the closed windows. Rays of light from the outside world splintered through their boards to form vivid stepping stones across the barn floor. The squares of light, Laurie noted, all seemed to form a path that led straight to the fire.

Royce grabbed Laurie's hand. "Come, Mother."

As Laurie took a step forward, she immediately felt a familiar sensation under her feet. She looked down to see snow covering the ground. She must have been too mesmerized by the barn to notice it when she first walked inside. She had little time to entertain the thought before a light tug from Royce kept her moving forward. When they were a few feet away from the flames, Royce stopped and faced her. Without a moment's hesitation, he gave her a reassuring smile and whispered, "I believe in you."

The words were like kerosene being poured onto the fire. In a blinding flash, the flames exploded to all corners of the barn, licking every wall, every beam, every square inch of snow. Then, as quickly as they had erupted, they retreated back to their small circular enclosure on the ground. Laurie barely had time to shield her eyes before the small campfire was burning again.

She turned to Royce for an explanation, but her words fell short.

All around her, clouds of mist began rising from the snow. They rose individually, yet they all shared the same chemistry. The clouds wafted in the air, sinking and falling gracefully. It reminded Laurie of when she had taken Royce to look at the jellyfish exhibit at the aquarium. He had marveled at the way the jellies were able to float aimlessly, as if in slow motion, while at the same time propelling themselves through the water. The mists appeared the same way, effortlessly floating in the sea of the barn.

But something else was floating with them. Laurie took a step toward the mists to get a better look. An image had begun to appear within the transparent fog. She concentrated harder, unable to blink at the mirage in front of her. The image materialized further and further until . . . *there*. She could see it.

The picture was of her as a child, no more than four or five years old.

She was playing in a sand box, laughing as she scooped up sand with a bucket and threw it in the air. Laurie stepped back and took in a full panorama of the barn. Images had begun to appear in every mist that rose from the ground beneath them. They were all glimpses of her childhood—all illustrating a different memory of her life. Some she recognized, and some she didn't, but they were all there. Every moment, every event, every breath. She could feel it. There were dozens and dozens of them, all roaming free.

She reached out to touch one, but her hand slid directly through the phantom depiction of herself. She immediately felt vulnerable, aware that there was no way to prevent the scenes from being displayed. She didn't understand why, but the very sight of them sent a wave a nausea over her body. Royce was the only other person in the barn, yet she felt like the entire world was seeing a snapshot of her life.

Laurie turned to her son. "What is this place?"

"This is the place He has allowed me to bring you. The place you need to go in order to find peace."

Laurie motioned to the rising mists around her. "But what is all of this?"

Royce held one of the images in place, analyzing its texture and appearance. Then, he sent it away with a light wave of his hand. The picture drifted away, getting lost in the congested traffic of memories. "This is you. *They* are you . . . from a particular era of your life."

"But why this age?" Laurie asked. "What do memories of me playing as a little girl have to do with my situation right now?"

"They have everything to do with your situation," replied Royce. "This is where it begins. This is where *you* begin."

"I don't understand."

"This is where you must regain your sight," said Royce plainly. "Like I told you before, we must look at the root of your suffering in order to find out where the healing must begin. This is the root. These pictures are where it all begins."

"This doesn't make sense. How do I regain my sight by simply looking at pictures of myself?" she asked.

"You will discover the answer shortly. But first, it will require something of you."

"And what is that?" Laurie asked.

"A prayer," said Royce. "But not just any prayer. Pain will not heal itself, so in order for the healing to begin, you must make a conscious choice to seek new vision."

"But I've already told you, Royce. I did what I did because I wanted the pain to disappear. I don't even know how to seek healing anymore."

Royce's face remained steadfast, his voice assured. "That's why I am here to help you, Mother. I told you that I would be with you every step of this journey."

Laurie looked at the clouds still swirling around her. She was learning to ride a bike, taking swim lessons, playing with Play-Doh. There and gone, image after image after image. She remembered her son's words, soft and kind and marked with a hint of desperation.

Please, Mother, for my sake . . .

She had promised him, and even though none of it made any sense, she would keep her word.

Laurie took a few seconds to compose herself, both aware and unaware of what she was committing to. After a few seconds, she spoke. "Okay, what is the prayer?"

"You already know it," replied Royce. "Close your eyes. It's there."

She did as she was instructed and closed her eyes.

At first, she saw nothing. She felt nothing. Moments crept by, but the only thing she was cognizant of was her own anxiousness. She hadn't even started the healing process, and she was already wishing it was over. Maybe Royce had finally gotten something wrong.

But then . . .

A jolt of energy surged through her body. Flashes of light scattered across the inside of her eyelids. As each streak entered and exited her vision, it left behind a speck of residue. After a few seconds, the residue collected together to form letters. Before long, a word appeared . . . then another . . . and another . . . until finally, an entire phrase. It wavered in front of her pupils as if it had been branded into her memory all along. It was clear, distinct, precise.

Laurie read the words out loud. "I pray I may, I pray I might, be shown how to heal, thus given new sight."

Chapter 12
A Picture Is Worth a
Thousand Wounds

As the last word leapt from Laurie's mouth, the clouds began to stir. At first they were lethargic, but they quickly picked up speed. Like a carnival ride building momentum, the memories hurled their way around the room, swooping and swirling as if on an invisible rollercoaster. They flashed around Laurie and Royce, swimming in front of them, behind them, above them, *through* them.

In the midst of the new chaos, Laurie's attention was drawn to the fire. Flames that were once sparkling white were now rippling with a variety of colors. And within those colors, another memory was being birthed. Little by little, it grew out of the flames and emerged into the air, rising eerily slow in comparison to the other clouds around it.

Once the mist reached eye level, it stopped rising and hung suspended in midair. Every other cloud inside the barn then sank to the ground and evaporated into the snow. Laurie didn't know what this particular memory held, but for the fact it was singled out meant that it had to be significant.

Immediately, the floating cloud expanded until it had engulfed the entire room.

Then, it stretched through the walls of the barn and swallowed them whole. Laurie and Royce had entered the picture, now bystanders in the theatre of her childhood. Laurie subconsciously pulled her son closer to her, linking her arm through his.

The clip on the screen began rolling forward.

The image displayed a dark room. Curtains were pulled across the windows to block most of the light, although a few rays of afternoon sun spilled out from around the edges. One didn't need much light to recognize that the room contained very little. A single dresser lay against the far wall with a TV sitting on top of it. Broken bunny ear antennas dangled loosely from the side of it, like untidy strands of hair. In the middle of the room, a man lie sleeping in a recliner next to an overturned coffee table. He was half-covered with a blanket and clutching a bottle. The smell of "too much to drink" pervaded the air.

The front door opened, and a small girl with dark brown pigtails came skipping inside. She hummed contently, mesmerized by a picture of a blue seahorse that she held in her hands. She closed the door and began to call out, but her words stopped abruptly when she saw the man in the recliner.

She quietly dropped her backpack to the floor and walked over to the chair. She raised her arm and nudged the man softly in the arm. "Daddy, are you okay? Hey . . . Daddy . . ." After a few more pokes, the man stirred awake and cast a dazed look at his daughter.

"Wha-what are you doing?" he asked, his words disoriented.

Most children would have been intimidated to wake their father up in that condition, but the young girl didn't appear to be fazed. It was as if she had experienced it before. She held up the picture to her father. "Look what I made at school today, Daddy. My teacher loved it, and I won first place. *And* I got a ribbon! It's in my backpack. Hold on, I'll get it. Here, look at the picture first."

The child beamed with joy as she handed her dad the picture and hurriedly searched in her backpack to find the ribbon. The man fumbled with the piece of paper, exerting more effort than necessary to figure out which way was right side up. Laurie slid her arm away from Royce as her face flushed in realization. "I know what this is—I remember it. This moment, the recliner, my father . . . I don't want to see it. Make it stop please."

Royce spoke calmly. "I'm sorry, Mother, but I cannot do that. We must watch it. It is vital to the healing process."

"But—"

"You asked to be shown how to heal, and now, He is showing you."

Laurie's tone grew more intense. "Yes, I know I said those words. I prayed it for you though. I didn't ask to watch my miserable childhood replayed before me. This isn't a lesson. This is tormenting a person with their past."

Royce looked at his mother, sympathetic, yet unwavering. "I'm so sorry. I told you this would not be easy, Mother. Nonetheless, we must continue."

Knowing that she would not be able to change Royce's mind, Laurie drew her eyes back to the screen that surrounded them.

Young Laurie hopped back to the recliner with a shiny pink ribbon in her hand. She placed it on the armchair with a proud grin. The man clumsily set the picture down and brought the ribbon to his face. As he did, he lifted the bottle to his mouth and took a shot, wincing as he swallowed. "I see there . . . very nice, Laurie."

She lit up at his words and leaned forward to point out something about the ribbon. But as she placed her hands on the armchair to boost herself up, the chair reclined and shot backwards. The bottle flew out of her father's hands and tumbled to the floor, sending golden liquid splashing everywhere. Laurie's picture lay drenched in a large puddle.

"Daddy, my picture!"

Laurie watched as her childhood self carefully tried to pick up the piece of paper from the floor. Tears welled in the young girl's eyes as she saw the colors blur and run down the page. Watching the scene, Laurie felt her own tears surfacing. They rose from a part of her that had never completely released the pain of that memory.

Young Laurie collapsed to the ground in complete devastation. "But it was my picture, and I worked so hard on it! It won first place, Daddy, and now it's ruined!"

Laurie's dad snatched the picture from her hands, instantly enraged. "Ruined? That's what you are worried about?" He tried to stand up too quickly and stumbled, catching himself on the wall. "Fussing over a damn picture! Get over it, Laurie. You're going to have a lot of disappointment in your life. That's just part of it."

Tears crawled down the young girl's cheeks as she sniffled again and again. "I did it for you though, Daddy. You were supposed to keep it and hang it on the fridge like the other parents do."

The man looked up and snarled. He picked the bottle up from the ground and drank what was left in it. Wiping his mouth with the back of his hand, he spat the words at his daughter. "I don't give a damn about what other parents do, Laurie. You hear that? Not a damn . . . What do they know? Shouldn't have woken me up while I'm sleeping anyway . . . Thinking I give a shit about a picture . . ."

"Daddy, you have drunk too much Coke," Laurie said whimpering. "I can smell it again. Please stop. Mommy said you aren't nice when you drink too much Coke." She began crying harder.

"Is that so? Well you know what, Laurie? I guess I'll just have to deal with her when she comes home as well. Now, get the hell out of here!"

He slung the bottle at the wall, shattering it above his daughter's head. Glass showered down on her, littering the floor. The man wadded up the picture and threw it across the room. Then, he lumbered into the kitchen, still swaying back and forth and muttering under his breath.

Young Laurie turned to run up the stairs, but her foot caught on her backpack. Crashing forward, she threw her hands out in front of her to catch her fall. A piece of glass shaped like a shark's tooth lodged deep into her palm. The scene began to shift, leaving a tiny girl balled up on blood stained carpet, her wails rupturing throughout the house . . .

The image dissolved into the fire, bringing the barn back into focus. There were no swirling clouds or floating pictures. Only the serene presence of the white flames and the peace that accompanied them.

Laurie held out her hand. The faint outline of a "V" scar stretched across her palm. A fit of anger flared inside her. "What did He want me to see out of that?" she asked harshly. "That my father was crazy? That he was a lousy drunk? That the apple doesn't fall far from the tree? Is that what He wants me to see?" She glared at her son, demanding answers, even though she knew he wasn't the one that should be responsible for providing them.

"Actually, that's exactly what He wants you to see," Royce responded.

"*What?*" Laurie said, astonished. "What are you talking about?"

Royce turned to face his mother. His voice was casual yet confident. "It is the first thing He wants you to recognize. Something that, while very basic in its concept, is the starting point for understanding your pain."

A cynical look clouded Laurie's eyes. "And what would that be?"

"*You must accept that some things are beyond your control.*"

Laurie's face drooped in disappointment. "That's it?" she said. "He had me relive a horrible memory from my childhood and experience that pain all over again, so that He could simply state the obvious?"

"Sometimes the answers we are looking for have the most obvious solutions, Mother."

Laurie scoffed, shaking her head. "I expected a new revelation, enlightenment, not Vacation Bible School answers. I thought He brought me to this place to show me things that I had never seen before? I know that some things are beyond my control. Don't you think I'm already aware of that fact?"

"You *claim* to be aware of that fact," Royce said quickly, "but being aware of a particular knowledge and actually applying that knowledge are two different things. Knowledge without application is useless. But the more important point is that you are only aware of that fact when it applies to other people."

"What do you mean?" Laurie asked, clearly annoyed.

"When things happen to other people that are beyond their control, we are quick to recognize it. We understand it, and we accept it. It's actually one of the ways that we try to comfort people, by trying to convince them that it wasn't their fault. That they were a victim who had no say in the outcome. When things happen to other people, we feel no bitterness or anger toward God. But isn't it interesting that when things happen to us *personally*, we ignore the knowledge that we claim to accept?"

Royce put his arms behind his back and began pacing around the fire. "Too many people hold on to pain that is beyond their control. They did not choose the pain, yet they allow it to shape their future. People have no control over where they are born, how they are born, or any other circumstance relating to it. I could have just as easily been born to a tribe in Africa or on a Native American reservation. I could have been born into extreme poverty or extreme wealth. Why are our cells born into the families in which they are born into? We have no control over that." Royce stopped walking, and his tone grew more serious. "It wasn't your fault that you were born into a broken home. It wasn't your fault that your dad was an alcoholic. It wasn't your fault that you were exposed to those things at that age."

"Royce, please," Laurie urged.

Royce persisted. "But somewhere down the road, you convinced yourself that you were no different, or any better, than your circumstances. You let the pain consume you. You let it transform you. You let it create a new identity for yourself."

"Royce, stop."

"If you accept that some things are beyond your control, then why are you bound by the very chains you claim to be free of?"

"*Stop!*" Laurie's voice echoed off of the barn rafters.

She backed away from the flame until she was under the balcony, as if its covering offered refuge from the storm inside of her. Silence spoke for the next few minutes as Laurie sorted through her own thoughts and regained control.

She stared at Royce across the fire. Her tone came out, not angry, but perplexed. "Why are you talking like this? You don't know anything about my life. You are—*were* too young, and there are things that you had no way of understanding."

"All knowledge is reborn in The World of White," Royce answered. "It's not my knowledge anymore, it's His. I no longer think the way I used to think because I no longer exist the way I used to exist. Once you arrive here, He changes you. And once He changes you, it's impossible to see things like you used to see them.

He allows me to know, and He allows me to understand, without the prejudice and biased attitude that would have otherwise blinded me from seeing the truth."

Laurie exhaled, unsure of what to say. A new fear prodded her mind: Royce could understand everything. He could see everything. This terrified her. She didn't want her son, her innocent and blameless son, to witness the unabridged version of her tortured life. She didn't want to be exposed for what she really was. At its core, it was too hurtful, too embarrassing, too real. Yet, she knew there was no way to control that he *could* understand and that he *would* see. To accept it would be to accept that everything was in the open. There were no more secrets. This too was beyond her control.

Royce had grown quiet by the fire, content with the silence and the flames. Laurie gazed at them as well, doing her best to allow the soft light to ease the ache in her heart. Finally, she spoke, her words filling the expanse of the room.

"You are right. I did let it transform me. I don't even know when it started . . . when I was young, obviously, but I don't know the exact moment."

"That's the way the *void* works," said Royce. "Once it is birthed, it festers in the cracks and crevices of our weaknesses, permeating throughout our lives in ways that we are not consciously aware of."

"What is the void?" Laurie asked.

"The void," Royce said deliberately, "is the space where people lose sight of *Him*. Where there should be love, there is hate. Where there should be joy, there is sorrow. Where there should be peace, there is unrest. Where there should be patience, there is haste. Where there should be humility, there is pride. And on and on and on. What He intended for good, the world intended for evil. When people do not make choices through Him, it creates a void of all that is whole and pure. Truth is removed. And if someone does not allow Him to fill the void, then it will continue from generation to generation until someone discovers freedom in Him again."

Laurie was not quite sure how the "void" directly applied to her life, or better yet, how it applied to things being beyond her control, but Royce continued unimpeded. "It goes by many names, most notably *sin*," he said, "but here we refer to it as the void."

"But how——" she began.

"Is it relevant to your situation?" Royce finished. "At some point, long before you were even born, your father made a choice to begin drinking. He drank to satisfy needs that human hands could never satisfy. The more he drank, the larger the void grew. Truth was removed farther and farther from his life. You were birthed into that void, automatically adopting it at an impressionable age. You were never aware of it, but it lay dormant inside of you because it was never properly dealt with. Since the seed had already been planted years before, it only took a little watering from tragedy, discouragement, and loneliness for your own void to grow. It was difficult to see where your father's void stopped and your own void began. All you knew is that somewhere things went wrong. The reality, however, is that the issue was rooted not in your own life, but in your father's life. And his choices were beyond your control."

Laurie nodded in acknowledgment.

"It does not excuse you from the poor choices you have made," Royce added. "But it does illustrate that the void birthed in your life was birthed in circumstances that were beyond your control. That's what He wants you to see."

"I blamed myself for everything," Laurie said. "For every temptation, every rejection, every drink. Even when I didn't understand why I felt that way, I still blamed myself. And then there came a point where I gave up trying to figure it all out. I let the shadows win. I became the very person that I had sworn to erase."

"That's why this first lesson is so important, Mother. We must rewire your thinking. You are not your father. You had no control over his choices, and therefore, you had no control over the person he would become. What you *do* have control over is using the void in your father's life as a means to eradicate the void in your own life. That is the root. That is where your healing begins."

"It doesn't seem that easy, Royce." Laurie's voice was dejected, broken. "It seems like it has been a part of me for so long that the thinking can't be rewired. There has simply been too much damage."

Royce acknowledged her comments, but his determined atti-tude did not falter. "If his choices were beyond your control, then the ability to fix those choices is beyond your control. That is the beauty of healing. You can't rewire anything, but you can allow Him to take control and rewire it for you. Recognizing it is the first step. He doesn't expect you to accept it immediately. This entire process is a journey. He understands that. You are aware that some things are beyond your control, but now it is time to *accept* that they are beyond your control. Then, you can begin to apply that knowledge in practical ways. It will take time, but the most important things always do."

It was only the first lesson, and already Laurie was feeling over-whelmed. It seemed impossible to register everything that Royce had just shared with her. She had subconsciously been aware of some of the principles he had discussed, but she had not consciously chosen to face them. Hearing her own son speak life into her had opened her mind to healing in a way that she had never experienced before. Still, she didn't know how she was going to endure through each of the lessons that lay ahead of her.

"My past is too much for me to relive one memory at a time, Royce. I'm not sure I can do this."

Royce joined his mother underneath the balcony. "You're right. You cannot do this . . . *alone*. That's why He has sent me to help you. There is so much beauty, Mother. So much freedom. And now, you get to experience it."

Chapter 13
The Sound of the Door

R oyce began to motion toward the fire, but as he opened his mouth to speak, Laurie interjected.

"Royce, I'm afraid . . . my past, it's . . ." She lowered her eyes in disgrace, unable to finish her sentence.

Royce spoke softly, as Laurie had spoken to him so many times before when he was little. "It's the only way, Mother."

"There must be another way," she insisted.

Royce shook his head regretfully. "We must fix the heart of the problem. Unfortunately, this is the only way it can be accomplished. You must have faith in the quality of who you are—the person you lost sight of long ago. That is where you will find the inner strength to endure through each memory. You have run for too long, Mother. The time for running is over. You are no longer a soul who retreats from a fight."

Once again, his words ignited the flames. They blasted into the air and illuminated the inside of the barn. Like a meteor passing through, the light wrapped its way around their bodies, making the world of the barn momentarily disappear. For a millisecond, Laurie thought that the pulsing light might never disappear—that it would seep into her skin and melt her bones; but the thought had hardly processed before the light subsided and caged itself back inside the campfire.

Laurie immediately looked at the surface of the snow, eager to see what the mists displayed this time; but nothing rose from the ground. In the first round, the mists had appeared instantly. So where were they now? Maybe there wouldn't be any other images? Laurie waited a few more seconds. Still nothing.

She turned to ask Royce if there had been a mistake, but as she opened her mouth, a small ghost cloud fell directly in front of her face. She jumped back in surprise.

She peeked out from underneath the balcony to try and see where it had come from. Cloud after cloud burst through the barn's ceiling, lowering themselves from the crossbeams of the rafters. Like large raindrops, they fell through the air and disappeared into the snow. Each of the mists were just as transparent as the last set, and each one contained a new image. They fell in endless supplies, a massive shower of memories whose source never dried up.

Laurie left the safety of the balcony and stepped into the open. The pictures on the mists were different than before. They no longer showed a young girl with cute pigtails riding a bike or coloring pictures. Laurie was older in these images. How much older, she couldn't say, but she was certainly in the next stage of her adolescence. One cloud showed her putting on lipstick and smacking her lips in the mirror. Another shot displayed her chatting noisily on the phone while looking at a comment someone had written in her yearbook.

But there was something else. Something . . . *off* about the clouds. At first, Laurie couldn't place it, but as she surveyed each passing image, it finally occurred to her. The mists were a shade darker than the last ones had been. She didn't know why that mattered, or if it even did matter, but there was no mistaking it. Their texture was no longer spotless and clean.

"Do you recognize these?" Royce asked.

"I'm a teenager. A young teenager."

"That's correct," he said. "It's a very important time period of your life." Royce's demeanor and tone of voice conveyed that he already knew every detail of this period of her life. It would have otherwise felt intrusive to Laurie, but she remembered what he had said about his knowledge in The World of White. "You know what you must do now," he added, more as an instruction than a question.

Yes, she knew, and she dreaded what would follow it. She tried to steady her breathing and prepare herself for whatever lay before her, but she knew that any real effort would be in vain. There never is a good way to prepare yourself for pain other than to face it head-on. Royce had already let her know that many times.

She attempted to speak with confidence, although her voice wavered. "I pray I may, I pray I might, be shown how to heal, thus given new sight."

The mists began swimming faster and in a much more chaotic pattern than before. The images picked up speed, rushing at Laurie like ghosts trying to intimidate her from ever returning to their hallowed arena. One after the next after the next. They flew by so quickly that Laurie could only catch a glimpse of what each picture contained. She felt like she was in a time warp preparing to transport to another galaxy.

Through the blur of images, Laurie saw the color of the fire once again transform. Navy, orange, crimson, violet—all there, flickering to life before her. The colors meshed together in an array of pixels, molding and shaping themselves to fit the same illustration. Once the picture was fully developed, it rose from the fire and floated gracefully into the air.

All the other images immediately froze in place, becoming a snapshot of still raindrops. The cloud above the fire started to move toward Laurie. As it did, each mist parted ways, creating a path for the cloud to travel. When it was roughly three feet from her face, it stopped moving. One by one, the other clouds rose steadily through the barn's rafters and out of sight. Laurie narrowed her eyes and peered into the single mist that hovered in front of her.

Seconds later, the picture elongated itself, stretching and reaching and pushing the boundaries of the barn until there was nothing left but the image itself. Laurie held her breath in anticipation. The clip of her life began playing.

Laurie's teenage self was lying on a bedroom floor next to a boy holding a tape recorder in his hands. As he pressed buttons on the recorder, the two squealed with laughter and shoved each other back and forth.

"I remember that toy," Laurie said to Royce. "We played with it for years. Troy was never really entertained by it, but Billy and I loved it. It was our favorite thing to do for fun." A tiny smile creased her lips as the memory spread its warmth around her.

But the warmth died quickly.

The corners of her mouth turned down in discomfort. "But there was one memory—" Understanding dawned on Laurie's face, and she grabbed her son. "Not this. Please Royce. You don't need to see this!"

"But I already have, Mother."

"Then I don't need to see this. I spent years trying to erase this image. I won't return to it. I *can't!*"

"But facing it is the only way to overcome it," Royce replied. "I know that while you are in the midst of the pain, it seems like it will never end. As if the pain will literally bleed you dry, like a towel ringing out every last drop of life. But it won't. Because through all of the mental and emotional agony, through all of the pain that refuses to subside despite pinching your eyes shut hoping it all goes away, through all of the emptiness left inside of you, one thing remains . . . air. You can still breathe, though labored and gasping and heavy, it's air nonetheless. And if you can breathe, then you are still alive. You must focus on one breath at a time. Feel the air fill your lungs and release again. *Over* and *over* and *over* again. And if you do this enough, then you will endure through these memories, Mother. I believe in you, and so does He."

Laurie wondered what it must be like to look upon someone else's pain and journey with them through each obstacle but never have to bear it yourself. She had experienced so much hurt in her life that she never really knew what it was like to be on the opposite end. The end that knew the answers and lived with peace because it had seen the hope that life could bring.

But there was more to it, she knew. When she looked in Royce's eyes, she didn't see someone who was pretending to sympathize with her. She saw something else. *Someone* else. It wasn't all clear yet, but maybe Royce felt more than she realized. She turned her attention back to the picture that continued to move forward.

The young boy spoke into the recorder, "Welcome back to our special show. It's one of a kind ladies and gentlemen, yes, one of a kind. We promised you the best, and by golly, that's what you'll get!"

Teenage Laurie giggled as he spoke, covering her mouth to try and muffle her laughter.

"We deliver breaking news to you, folks. The very minute it occurs!" The boy put two fingers to his ear, tapping an invisible earpiece. "Wait, what's this? A new story has just surfaced, even as we speak! We have just received word that Laurie has once again wet the bed. Yes, you heard me ladies and gentleman, she has peed—"

"Hey!" Laurie punched the boy in his arm. She reached over him to try and steal the recorder, but his arms were longer than hers. He held the recorder just out of her reach, speaking faster.

"Quite a mess. Comforter and all, folks, you heard me!"

"Let the record show," Laurie yelled into the recorder, "that Billy has dumped in the bathtub again. Yes, poop is floating everywhere!"

Billy shouted louder, "A tidal wave of pee, folks. All she needed was a bathing suit and a surfboard!"

Laurie, even louder, "Turds as big as icebergs! Could sink the *Titanic* folks!"

Both children shrieked with laughter. Then, Billy rewound the recording and switched the mode to "squeak." Their voices popped out sounding like Alvin and the chipmunks. This made the two kids wail even harder. They rolled on their stomachs and clutched their aching sides.

Slam!

The noise cut off their laughter.

Instinctively, Billy and Laurie scurried to the bedroom door and pressed their ears against it.

Even though Laurie and Royce were bystanders to the scene, Laurie remembered the emotions that she felt that night. She and her brothers could always tell their father's mood by the sound the door made when he came home from work. Every evening, they subconsciously prayed for the door to gently *click* shut and for their parents to embrace. But it didn't always work out like that. It was when the door slammed rather than clicked that they held their breath and

127

wished time would fast forward to the next day. Then the sun would rise, and the shadows would disappear.

That night, the door had communicated that it had been a rough day. As she watched in limbo, Laurie remembered thinking that maybe their father would be the lesser of evils that night. That maybe everyone would make it to the morning without any new scars. Maybe that night would be different, giving them a reason to think that it didn't always have to be bad.

Her young teenage self had clung to so many maybes.

"Dinner ready yet?" Their father's voice came out sounding brash. Accusing.

Drunk.

Their mother responded, too low for the kids to hear clearly. They jammed their ears into the door harder, trying to make out every word that was spoken. Laurie watched in bewilderment, remembering how they were always horrified at what they heard but how it had never stopped them from listening.

She whispered to Royce while the clip played on. "Troy was gone at a basketball camp that weekend. I still remember the terror that I felt, knowing that if something happened, he wouldn't be there to help. We always felt safer as siblings if we were all three together." Her words came out hollow, drifting away into the open air of the bedroom scene before them.

More comments were exchanged back and forth between Laurie's parents while the kids remained plastered against the door.

"I don't know what they will do, Elizabeth. I told you every-thing that they told me. It's out of my hands now . . ."

A chair scratched across the floor, most likely their father bump-ing into it. He cursed.

Their mother said something. The kids strained further, their faces growing red from holding their breath to listen. Even though their mother's responses were always a bit too muffled for them to understand, their father's voice was loud enough to let them know the gist of the conversation.

"What do you want me to say? It was a hard day, and I needed to unwind . . . Well, you just keep on thinking that then . . . No, that's all you ever talk about, so go ahead and believe it . . . Like you have nothing to do with it? Like it's all *my* responsibility?"

This time, they didn't need to strain to hear their mother's reply. "Yes, it's *your* responsibility! This isn't about your boss, or the layoffs, or how I take care of the kids. All of those things are just excuses for you to hide behind because you can't face reality. But you're right, maybe an empty bottle is more important than your fami—"

Smack!

The sound echoed throughout the barn. Laurie cringed and grabbed for Royce's hand. She squeezed her eyes shut, but the same image floated into her mind that was currently playing before her. She still remembered that sound. The way her father's slap had vibrated off the walls of their house. The way her mother's cry had vibrated off the walls of her heart. The reality was suddenly too real. She hugged Royce closer.

Their father's words were tenacious. "I'm not going to sit here and listen to your bullshit. Now, get up . . . I said, get *up!*"

Glass shattered, and their father's wails splintered the room.

"Bitch!" he screamed. The next few moments were filled with the sound of shuffling feet and bodies grappling together as furniture crashed around the room.

Beside Royce, Laurie shuddered in a cold sweat. Years after the incident, her mother had talked to her about what happened that night. She told Laurie that when their father had reached for her, she had broken a glass bowl over the side of his head. It was the first time that she had really stood up to him before. It could have been, *should* have been, a moment of pride, a small victory, if not for the way the night had ended.

On the screen, Billy slung open the bedroom door and stormed out.

"Billy, no! Stop!" Laurie hurled herself at him, but her small arms slid off his waist as he rounded the corner. She crumpled to the floor, the living room now visible from around the bedroom door-frame. Her father had one hand around her mother's throat and the other hand raised in the air.

"Stop!" Billy yelled. His voice was loud, but his legs were visibly shaking.

Their father's arm paused in midair. He shot around and glared at Billy. "Well, look who wants to be a hero."

"Let her go," Billy said defiantly. His jaw was set, and his fists were clenched in expectation. He was already breathing fast, his chest expanding and contracting rapidly. Their father looked at Billy as if he was impressed by his courage, nodded, and relaxed his grip on their mother's throat. For a brief moment, it seemed that things might be all right.

Their mother scrambled over to Billy. "Go back to the room baby. Leave mom and dad to talk." Her left eye was already starting to swell, and her lip was cut. Billy didn't budge.

"No, Mom," he said. "I won't let him touch you."

"That's right, Liz," said their father. "He won't let me touch you." An eerie smile formed on his lips. "So I guess he'll just have to take your place."

"No, Cal, please!" She ran to her husband and clutched his arm desperately, but she was defenseless against his strength. He tossed her aside like a ragdoll.

Billy lunged at his father, attempting to tackle him at his waist. Cal scoffed and grabbed a handful of Billy's hair. He shoved his head back hard, sending Billy hurtling to the floor.

"Cal, I'm begging you! He's just a boy. Don't do this!" She had started crying now, panic in her voice and hopelessness in her eyes.

Cal ignored his wife. "This boy needs to be taught a lesson about respect, Liz. This will be the last time he decides to pull a stunt like this." Billy got back to his feet, determined. He reared back and swung as hard as he could, hitting his dad right in the gut. A low *mmph* escaped Cal's mouth as his breath was knocked out. But it did little damage. Perhaps a grown man's punch would have taken him down, but Billy was still a boy. The hit only enraged his father further. His hand veered around, smacking Billy across the face. Billy collapsed to his knees, struggling to stay upright. Elizabeth shrieked in hysteria. Sobbing, she gathered every last bit of strength that she had and threw herself at her husband. But even that was not enough to stop the nightmare that was occurring. One hit later, Elizabeth lay on the ground unconscious.

Tears of hatred pooled in Billy's eyes. He gritted his teeth and scrambled toward his father's legs. He grasped them with all his might and bit into his father's thigh. Cal howled in pain. He dropped to the floor, the thud rattling the pictures in the living room and the dishes in the kitchen. Billy shot to his feet with renewed vigor.

But as he charged at his father again, Cal reached for a marble vase that sat on the coffee table beside him. Billy didn't see it coming until it was too late. He had no time to react. Cal smashed the vase into Billy's left leg, shattering his kneecap.

Laurie shot her head away and buried it into Royce's shoulder. The sound of her brother's bones crunching had been a ghost that she had fought hard to destroy. She had never quite been able to accomplish it. She didn't need to watch anymore. She knew all too well how the scene played out after that.

Her father rose to his feet, wiped his face with his forearm, and walked out of the house. The door slammed behind him, leaving Billy lying on the ground lifeless in a pool of his own blood.

Flames from the small fire ate the memory, returning everything in the barn to its appropriate place.

"It's not fair," Laurie said, breaking the silence. There was no hint of sadness, just blatant fury. "Why did I have to see that? What was the point of that?"

"To hea—"

"To heal, yeah, I know," Laurie interrupted. "So what did He want me to see this time? Because it looked like the same as before. Lousy drunk. Terrible father. Abusive husband. Is this what you mean by healing? To see the same thing over and over and over again?"

"No, Mother—" Royce started.

"It wasn't my fault. Got it. Some things are beyond my control. Covered it. We have already seen that. We have already seen that. We have already SEEN THAT!" Laurie screamed into the rafters, her words sharp and stinging. Royce remained still, waiting for the echo of her words to die away.

"You are right," he said finally. "Your father's choices were beyond your control. But that is not what He wants you to see here."

"Well, what is it then?" Laurie demanded.

"Forgiveness," replied Royce.

Laurie erupted. "Forgiveness? *FORGIVENESS?* He never asked for forgiveness! He never asked for anything other than another drink, or his next fix, or the woman across the street!"

Laurie knew that her son wasn't to blame, but he was sent to her by the one who *was* to blame for it all. She couldn't help coming unraveled.

"I am not speaking of whether or not he asked for forgiveness." Royce squeezed her hand, as if hinting at the true meaning behind his words. "This isn't about your father or his choices. He was obviously in no position to think rationally. This was never about him. This is about you. That is what He wants you to see from this picture. *You must forgive others and surrender your pain.*"

Laurie shook her head adamantly. "Why would I forgive someone who I have spent my entire life trying to forget? He was drunk every other night. He severely abused my brothers and my mom. He ruined any chance we had at having a normal family. I wouldn't even know where to start . . ."

"Actually, those are perfect places to start," Royce said. "Often, what we find ridiculous, He finds redemptive. Your subconscious already knows the pain that thrives at the core of your being. Those issues are the very things that you must embrace."

Laurie laughed sarcastically and dropped Royce's hand. She began walking toward the barn door, still shaking her head. "That's just the thing, you make it sound so easy. Like it happens with the flip of a switch."

"He knows that life doesn't work that way," Royce called out after her. "What He wants to do is bring things out of the shadows into the light. Once you have the motivation to change, then He will help instill in you the discipline that you need to continue to change. That discipline is only developed over weeks, months, and even years of practice. Please don't reject the solutions He offers simply because you think they are offered flippantly."

Laurie stopped walking. "Even if I was willing to try and heal one day at a time, there is something that you are overlooking. He doesn't *deserve* to be forgiven, Royce."

And he didn't. When Laurie looked back on her father's life, there were few good things he *did* deserve. He had been his own worst enemy. He had created his own demons. Time after time, he had placed himself in a position to fail. He had done all of those things, not her. Laurie didn't think she should have to carry that burden and accept that it was all fine. That's what forgiveness was, wasn't it? Giving people a free pass from all of the terrible things they had done? Not this time. She wasn't handing out free passes to anyone.

Laurie lifted both hands to pull open the barn doors.

"So you should have been in complete control over whether he lived or died?"

Laurie hesitated, her fingers gripping the wood. "What are you talking about?" she asked defensively.

Royce's voice was voluminous, carrying over time and space to fill the silent void that hung between them. "To say that your father does not deserve forgiveness is to imply that he deserves to be condemned. And to claim who is worthy of forgiveness and who is worthy of condemnation is to determine the fate of their soul. It's the claim that you know how they were knit together inside their mother's womb, and that you know every fiber of their being, every emotion they have ever felt, every thought they have ever constructed, and every purpose they have yet to fulfill. It's the claim that you fully grasp and comprehend those intricate details and are willing to make a judgement of whether or not they are deserving of an abundant life. Is that where you have landed yourself? Someone who possesses all wisdom and all knowledge and is qualified to determine whether or not someone lives or dies? Whether someone should be extended grace or sentenced to suffer for all eternity?"

Laurie didn't know what to say. She had never considered those things. It didn't seem fair that Royce would put that on her. Obviously, he knew more than she did in this place. But he was right, wasn't he? She was in no position to judge whether someone deserved mercy or punishment. And if she wasn't qualified to judge other people, then what made judging her father any different? Was it because he was *her* father and his decisions had impacted *her* personally, so she felt entitled to judge him as she pleased?

Laurie let go of the door and turned to face Royce. He was standing as he always did, his demeanor as it always was, nonthreatening. Half of his face was lit by the fire, and half of his face was masked by the shadows. It was symbolic of what he had become to Laurie. One side was a boy she had loved and raised and cherished, while the other side contained a spirit that unveiled every secret she had ever possessed. She didn't know that side at all, but that side knew her completely. This awareness was unnerving.

Royce continued talking, lowering his voice again as if they were in an intimate conversation. "Forgiveness is not connected to entitlement. If forgiveness was only bestowed to the ones who deserved it, then no one would receive mercy. We all deserve to face an afterlife of agony and misery and damnation. It is one of the cornerstones of why we believe what we believe. We are all broken people, which is why we are in desperate need of a savior. You must understand this, Mother. We don't forgive based off of who deserves it. That's not our job, not our burden. It's *His*. All we must do is what is required of us, which is to forgive. It is a very important step in the healing process."

Royce motioned with his arm, and Laurie reluctantly made her way back to him. She positioned herself on the opposite side of the fire, a subtle maneuver to maintain her distance for the time being. She was still unsure of how to process everything—what she agreed with and what she didn't agree with.

"He wouldn't have accepted it," she said, her eyes downcast. "It would have been pointless. And now he's gone, so it is useless to consider anyway."

"Oh, but, Mother, it isn't!" Royce spoke with renewed energy. "These are all conditional ways of thinking. Whether or not someone deserves it, how they will respond, if the timing is right, if it's too late . . . all conditional. You don't forgive people conditionally. You forgive them unconditionally. You forgive, not for what it does *for* them, but for what it does *in* you." His eyes sparkled, the reflection of the flames always present in them. "Forgiving others sets us free from our own chains of bitterness."

Laurie nodded, contemplated a moment, then responded. "You said that you must forgive others and surrender your pain. Explain the second part . . . *surrender your pain*. What do you mean by that?"

Royce acknowledged the question. "We have all heard that we need to forgive, but we often don't understand the implications of what that means. People will claim that they have forgiven others, but they choose to remain tortured by the pain that those people have caused them. They latch on to anger, bitterness, and resentment. Like a plague, they allow those things to infect their daily lives. They simply won't give in and acknowledge that their pride is causing their own destruction. To surrender your pain is to yield that pain to a higher authority. It's saying that you are going to submit to Him and allow Him to remove the burden from you because the burden is no longer your own. It means offering your pain to Him with open hands. It means abandoning yourself entirely to accept His peace. You see, Mother, to say the right words is to forgive with your mouth, but to surrender your pain is to forgive with your heart. . . one day, one breath at a time."

A few moments passed, the flicker of the flames creating a soothing ambience as Laurie considered Royce's words.

"We always told you that your Uncle Billy hurt his knee playing football his senior year of high school. We didn't think those were details that you needed to know for a long time, if ever. I guess we are beyond that now." Laurie's face looked deflated, weary from emotion and mental fatigue. "I don't know how all of this pieces together, or to what end. I'm not sure if I am even *alive*, Royce. But it would take a lot of time to move on and heal from all of this."

Royce nodded in agreement. "Of course healing takes time, Mother, but there is one thing you cannot overlook. We must first make the choice to take action, then we can allow His process to work through us. Choose to accept that some things are beyond your control, then learn how to apply that knowledge to find peace. Choose to forgive, then learn how to surrender your pain one day at a time. We must first determine that there is no going back—no matter what it costs, no matter what part of us is left vulnerable, no matter what we are forced to leave behind, no matter what the world thinks of us. We *must* make that choice. Once we do, then the healing can truly begin."

Chapter 14
Water and Blood

"I know at this point, things seem daunting. Unanswered questions still linger. Emotions are worn raw. He understands what you are experiencing, and He hates to see you in pain. He wants you to know that every lesson you learn here is not in vain, and every tear you cry is not discarded. He asks that you be strong again, Mother. This next image reaches to the core of who you are. It will affect you in a far greater way than the previous images you have seen."

Royce and Laurie were watching dark clouds swirl in angry knots. Their color had transitioned into a deep purple, certainly more menacing than all of the mists before them. In the center of the room, so many pictures clashed together that it was difficult to see the other side of the barn. It seemed like they were unleashing their wrath on each other, like an aggravated hive of bees. Laurie could sense that whatever they held was dark and tormented.

"There is so much pain in these scenes," Laurie said. "I believe what you have told me, but how am I expected to endure through these without any other explanation as to their overall purpose?"

"I have told you their overall purpose," Royce replied. "There are no games here, Mother. His only goal, only focus, only intention, is your healing."

"Yes, my healing." Laurie cast her eyes to the ground. "I thought you would say that." The images flew by in quick bursts, barely giving her time to see what lay within them. She caught sight of bits and pieces . . . her pinning stars to her letterman jacket, a group of friends cheering at a homecoming football game, a picture of her first kiss. They swept by in clusters, all illustrating what Laurie recognized as her late teen years. "I'm sorry, Royce. I wish I was stronger. I wish I could endure better."

"It's not about how *well* we endure. It's that we endure. Sometimes, that's all He asks of us." The confidence in his voice never seemed to waver, and his focus never seemed to falter.

Laurie was taken back to the day of Royce's funeral, standing over his casket while the rain poured down around them. The memory was like a lightning bolt striking at her conscience, reminding her of her failure as a mother. The suffering he must have endured while she had been caring only for herself . . . simply unbearable. She had made so many mistakes, but now she had an opportunity to do something right—even if that something was not done well. She knew that she could not give up. She would endure for Royce.

Laurie took a few deliberate breaths and called out to the images. "I pray I may, I pray I might, be shown how to heal, thus given new sight."

Immediately, an array of colors sparked from the fire and thrust an image into the air. It was quickly swept up into the heart of the mists that swarmed together. The entire pile of clouds began vibrating. Despite the chaos already present, it was obvious that the newcomer was not welcome. The images started shaking faster and faster.

Laurie held her breath in anticipation. And then it happened.

The entire mass of pictures exploded, sending dark clouds hurtling through all sides of the barn. Laurie ducked out of instinct, momentarily forgetting that the clouds could not physically harm her. When she looked up again, the image that had risen from the fire was left floating by itself. She stood up straight again. The cloud didn't wait to see if Laurie was paying attention. It started growing larger and larger until the barn was seized by the memory.

The clip had barely moved forward before the strength in Laurie's legs gave out. She collapsed to the ground.

Deep within her subconscious, she had known this memory would appear somewhere. The incident had stripped away too much of her sanity and had numbed too many of her emotions to stay dormant for long. It was always there, waiting, stalking. And now she would face it again. She glanced at the scene that loomed around them, hoping that what Royce said was true and that everything happening was not in vain.

A group of students poured out of a gymnasium into its parking lot, chatting loudly and motioning with excitement. All of their attention was focused on a tall boy in the middle of the pack. He was drenched in sweat and had an athletic bag thrown over his shoulder. They hugged and congratulated him, tussling his hair and offering him playful shoves.

The group finally said goodbye to each other and dispersed across the parking lot. The tall boy was left standing with a girl beside him. She threw her arm around his shoulders and began guiding him toward a car at the end of the row.

"You don't have an option," she said. "We are hitting up Gary's Diner with everyone. You can't let down your adoring fans." She smirked at him and grabbed her keys out of her purse.

The boy rolled his eyes, smiling. "Whatever . . . it's fine, really. I don't have the money anyway. We will grab something at the house."

"Are you kidding? After a game like that? Nope, I won't accept it. Meal's on me this time, big boy. You earned it . . ."

The boy laughed and shrugged away the comment, "You don't have to do that, Laurie. It's not that big of a deal."

"It's the least that I can do . . . after all, what kind of sister would I be if I didn't take care of my little brother?" She winked at him as they climbed into the car.

"Three minutes. Younger by three minutes," he sighed.

"Troy, every minute counts," she retorted quickly.

"Fine," he said with a cheesy grin. "Then, I'll be ordering one of everything. Hope you're ready."

"Well, the sky's the limit," she said, "up to five dollars and twenty-five cents."

"I knew there was a catch."

"Always a catch," she laughed. "Girl's gotta have gas money to get to work tomorrow you know." She rolled down the windows and turned up the radio as they pulled out of the parking lot and veered onto the street.

"This calls for some celebrating," he said loudly over the music. "Open the sunroof!"

"Not yet, Troy!" Laurie protested. "Wait until we get over Junction Row. You know how those curves scare me."

"Put on your big girl pants. You're fine!"

"Oh, please. I'm the one who convinced you to start doing that to begin with." The car rumbled up a small hill, disappearing around a blind curve.

"Laurie the Legend, brave enough to toilet paper the principal's house but too scared to let in some fresh air," he picked.

"Really? You are going there? So unfair."

"Admit it, you love this drive. It's scary but fun."

"I won't admit that," she said stubbornly.

Troy beat the ceiling of the car. "Sun-roof! Sun-roof!"

"No!"

"Sun-roof! Sun-roof!" he chanted.

"Can't hear youuuu!" Laurie said louder.

Troy erupted. "SUN-ROOF! SUN-ROOF!"

"OKAY!" she burst. "Just because it's your big night . . . I love you, but sometimes I want to strangle you."

"Only sometimes." Troy smiled.

Laurie shook her head and opened the sunroof. She crossed her arm in front of her, bowing humbly. "Anything for you, my liege."

Seconds later, Troy's torso was sticking out of the top of the car. His wavy hair flowed with the wind as he threw his arms up and cheered. Laurie swerved purposefully hard around one turn, making Troy snort with laughter.

"Turn this song up!" he yelled down to her.

She reached for the volume.

The man was wearing all black, his silhouette camouflaged against the night sky surrounding him. He stumbled into Laurie's lane as she turned her eyes to the radio. Troy's scream snapped her attention back to the road. She jerked the wheel frantically to the left, swerving into the next lane. She could hear Troy grappling with the roof, desperately trying to hang on. The car was headed straight for the opposing guardrail until Laurie locked the breaks and yanked the wheel again. If it hadn't been for gravel on the shoulder of the road, they would have just cleared the railing.

If.

Laurie's back tires lost traction and clipped the guardrail. The car careened out of control, spinning across the road. Troy's body thrashed back and forth on the roof, helpless as the car skated over the side of an embankment. The vehicle barrel rolled several times, a mixed blur of glass and flesh and metal and earth. It finally came to rest on its side in a mangled heap.

Thunder clapped, and small drops of rain pelted the scene. Water and blood intersected each other, trickling down the shattered windshield. All lay still, inside and outside of the car, as the scene lifted.

Royce walked around the fire and knelt beside his grieving mother. Her tears fell long and hard, each one making a small indention in the snowy ground as they landed. It was several minutes before she spoke again.

"He was my best friend," she said weakly. "I remember waking up in the hospital and seeing Billy and my mom sitting beside my bed. They were both crying. I was still disoriented, but even then, I knew." Laurie stared at her open hands, rubbing the v-scar in her palm. Her voice was distant, clearly lost in the memory of that night. "The doctor took my mother's hands in both of his and just squeezed them. I saw his mouth moving but struggled to focus on his voice. I do remember one thing he said though, right before I passed out again. He said, 'I'm so sorry for your loss. Sometimes in life, when it rains it pours.'"

"I'm sorry that you had to experience that, Mother," Royce said. Laurie could feel the compassion in his voice. She still did not understand how he could speak to her like that, as if he had been in the seat next to her while the car took her twin brother's life. He spoke as if he still felt the pain of that night in the same way she did.

Laurie remained on the ground, staring aimlessly into the fire. "Later, the police would tell us that the man had been drunk that night. Apparently, he had no recollection of how far he had stumbled into our lane. It was just . . . so terrible. A nightmare that never ended."

"That's one reason th—"

"To this day," Laurie continued, "I still wonder why I lived and he died. I remember hearing news stories in high school of people who had experienced similar things, and I remember thinking how horrible it would feel to be in that position. Then it happened to me. I knew then, that I had been clueless about what true horror felt like . . . why did I deserve to live, Royce?"

Royce repositioned himself on the ground next to her. "It's important to see things through the proper lens. He does not see matters as deserving or undeserving, as if you were better than your brother or deserved life more than he did. There is merely the truth. What happened that night—"

"Was my fault," interjected Laurie. "My blame. My guilt."

"No, that's not how He sees it," said Royce. "It is not in His nature to see things that way."

"It doesn't matter," Laurie whimpered. "I can't go back and put myself in that car again. I can't go back and refuse to let my brother hang out of the sunroof. I can't go back and not reach for the radio. I can't . . ."

"And that, Mother, is why this lesson is so important," Royce reinforced. He tenderly stroked her hair. "It is one of the most difficult challenges and one of the most difficult aspects of the healing process."

"What is it?" asked Laurie.

"The last lesson and this lesson are closely linked. In the last lesson, you were reminded that you must forgive others and surrender your pain. Now, he wants you to see that *you must forgive yourself and release your pain.*"

"I have tried to forgive myself, and it hasn't worked too well," said Laurie.

"That's because you have never really learned how to forgive yourself," replied Royce. "Many people claim that they are 'working on forgiving themselves,' but if you unwrap that, what they often mean is that they have become mired down with mediocre living.

They have grown satisfied with meeting the status quo. Surviving rather than *thriving*. They technically haven't 'given up,' so they think this wins them a moral victory. While it is good to focus on living one day at a time, with this attitude, you aren't making an intentional choice to forgive yourself. You are simply hanging on and hoping that things get better. The reality is that things won't get better until we make a conscious decision to make them better."

"I think there is some truth to that though, that some people just need time. You don't think that time can heal wounds?" Laurie asked.

"*Intentional* time can heal wounds," Royce corrected.

"But it's still a process. So, how do you live with the pain in the meantime? Considering that the pain will never erase completely?"

Royce rose to his feet. "You are implying that in order to completely forgive yourself the pain must no longer exist," said Royce. "But that's not correct. The ability to forgive yourself is something you develop in spite of the pain, not in the absence of the pain."

"And how do you do that?" Laurie persisted.

"There are no simple answers, Mother. I want to remind you that just because these principles will quickly be discussed in the time we have together, it does not mean that they will quickly be accomplished. I recognize that, and so does He." Laurie acknowledged it, and Royce continued, "You must understand the power of winning daily battles, the evidence of unconditional grace in your life, and the significance of living in the present."

"What do—"

"I'll explain each one," Royce affirmed. "These are simple truths. Vital, but simple. First, winning daily battles." Royce put his arms behind his back and casually paced back and forth, as if delivering a lecture to a class. "People misinterpret the effort it takes to forgive yourself. They view forgiveness, forgiving someone else as well as forgiving yourself, as a singular event. A onetime decision. A decision that, once made, makes the symptoms of pain, grief, guilt, and shame, all disappear. The assumption is that the eradication of the symptoms is directly linked to the decision to forgive. Sadly, that's not how it works."

"Then how does it work?" Laurie asked.

"You must wake up each day and recommit to forgiving yourself. It is not a onetime fix. It is a daily fix. Accepting that some things are beyond your control, learning to forgive others, learning to forgive yourself, maintaining the right mind-set, being at peace with yourself—all require daily commitments."

"It doesn't seem that easy though," Laurie mused. "If it were that easy, then most people wouldn't struggle with the decision."

"Most people struggle with the decision because they do not understand the decision. To wake up day after day, committing to the same choice, takes mental and emotional discipline. That kind of discipline is not easy, which is a key part of the problem. Society wants solutions that are fast, easy, comfortable, and convenient. Often, the issue is not that people cannot forgive themselves, it's that they do not want to put forth the time and energy it takes to forgive themselves. But there is something else, though. Something much more encouraging."

"What's that?" Laurie asked.

"It does get easier. For example, if you are trying to form a new habit, a healthier diet, let's say, it will be frustrating at first. You may repeat the process day after day, week after week, without seeing any results. You might find that the temptation to return to your old habits is still there and doesn't seem to be getting any easier to deal with. But then one day, things change. You don't know exactly when it happened, but you find yourself able to cope with things better, make wiser choices, and stay disciplined without as much mental turmoil. More time goes by, and before you know it, you rarely have to try hard because those new habits are a part of your lifestyle. Will you occasionally see something that will tempt you to veer off track? Of course. The temptation to return to an old lifestyle will never disappear completely. But once you have developed a new mind-set, then you are able to control those emotions more effectively. Not to oversimplify it, Mother, but it will get easier. You just have to be willing to go to the effort to fight for it."

Laurie nodded, still sitting in the same position on the ground. She had barely looked up the entire time Royce had spoken.

Royce finished. "If you decide once, then you haven't decided at all. It must be a daily mind-set. You must wake up each morning and determine that your future will not be determined by your past. Accomplish that, and you will begin to see the power that comes from winning daily battles."

"I don't even know where to begin thinking like that," Laurie replied.

"I understand, Mother. With most of these lessons, the key is learning how to rewire your thinking. It will be difficult to grasp at first, but it is a crucial step in your journey, as is the next point."

"Unconditional grace," Laurie said.

"Yes, unconditional grace." Royce smiled. "Forgiveness implies grace. When you forgive someone, you are showing a measure of grace to that person. Likewise, if you refuse to forgive yourself, then you are refusing to show grace to yourself. Essentially, you are condemning yourself. What's important, however, is that the one who sent me has not condemned you. He has redeemed you. He has granted you unconditional grace."

"What if I can't accept that though?" asked Laurie. Her voice was heavy, as if each of Royce's words were draining more and more energy from her.

"If you cannot accept that, then you are confiding more in your selfishness than in His *selflessness*. You would be claiming that your judgment is more powerful than His mercy. That is completely twisted. If He does not condemn us, then we have no right to condemn ourselves. The key is maintaining that mind-set, which is a daily, intentional decision."

"You said that I needed to forgive myself and *release* my pain," Laurie said. "Explain how extending myself grace is directly linked to releasing my pain."

"Of course," Royce said. "Too often, people cling to their pain as if they are trying to protect it; like it is one of their most sacred possessions. The notion of releasing something signifies that you are no longer holding it captive. You are allowing it to escape from confinement. When you choose to live in grace, you allow the pain to move, to be set free. And when you set your pain free, you set your spirit free. I know it seems impossible now, but you'll see, Mother. As you learn to forgive yourself, you will also learn how to loosen the grip on your pain and experience true liberation."

"I'm not sure I can do that," said Laurie. Her voice cracked beneath the weight of her emotions. "I think a part of me will always look back, will always regret what I did."

Royce took his place beside Laurie once more.

"Let me tell you a story. It's a story that I actually heard from Pastor Scoggins during Vacation Bible School one year. While the story itself is fictional, it helped me understand forgiveness better. Maybe it will help you as well."

Laurie remained silent, and Royce continued. "There was a pastor of a church who was haunted by a mistake he had made in college. For years, he had battled with the regret, the guilt, and the shame. On several occasions, he had even asked his congregation to forgive him, but that had brought him little peace. One day, an elderly lady from the congregation claimed that she could talk to God and that He would audibly answer her. Week after week, she returned to the church and told the other members about her lengthy conversations with God. The pastor grew weary of her claims and finally decided to test them.

"He said to her, 'If you can really talk to God, then go home and ask Him what mistake I made years ago that I have yet to forgive myself for.'

"She smiled and assured the pastor she would do just that. The following Sunday, the lady returned and approached the pastor.

"'Did you talk to God?' the pastor questioned.

"The lady acknowledged that she had indeed talked to Him.

"'Did you ask Him about the mistake I made years ago?' he asked.

"She nodded, affirming that she had.

"'What did he say?'

"The lady smiled. 'He said, "I can't remember."'"

Laurie sobbed quietly. Royce reached down and tilted her chin up, connecting their eyes. "Mother, this story illustrates the beauty of the third point—the significance of living in the present. Because of His grace, we have the opportunity to wake up each day and start over. Each sunrise offers us a chance to see the world differently, to change, to leave the past in the past. If you are too focused on the pain behind you, then you won't recognize His purpose in front of you. You can, and must, be fully invested in *this* day . . . in the pursuit of the abundant life that He has for you. You have enslaved yourself with chains in the past, but He has come to set you free in the present. Take hope in *today*."

Royce wrapped his arms around his mother and swayed her gently. Laurie didn't speak because too many thoughts were fighting for control of her mind, and Royce didn't speak because he knew that his mother needed to win that fight. Silence enveloped them as the fire continued to cackle and burn.

Chapter 15
A Dozen Anniversaries

"This journey is almost finished, but I'm afraid that these last two lessons are ones that could prove to be the most painful. I know that may seem harsh after all that you have endured, but there is no other way to bypass the pain. There are no shortcuts. Just remember, Mother, when you have finished the journey, healing *will* occur. He promises it, and His promises never fail. I hope somewhere deep inside, you can grasp that truth."

Laurie nodded mechanically. No matter how hard he had tried to prepare her, it hadn't sufficed to what she had encountered already. Everything that she had experienced had overwhelmed her thinking and numbed her emotions. At this point, there was only one thing that kept her moving forward: the promise she had made to Royce that she would not give up.

As if he saw the fight in her eyes, he whispered, "Thank you."

A single spark shot out from the fire and dissolved into the snow. Then, another spark, bigger this time, *popped* and vanished into the air. One-by-one, sparks were tossed from the fire, snapping and fizzling. With each spark, Laurie noticed that the flames leapt a bit higher. A bit wider.

The fire was growing.

The white tongues snatched at the air, propelling themselves higher into the vastness of the barn. Laurie backed away, edging under the balcony for protection. She knew that Royce would not allow her to be harmed, although the look and size of the fire was still intimidating. It stretched further until Laurie thought that the ceiling might catch ablaze.

The tension finally broke, and white flames burst in every direction, leaving in their wake clouds of memories. Mists that were once dark shades of purple were now swirling mixtures of charcoal and black. But they no longer just looked different, they also influenced the environment around them. Laurie could sense it. Their presence automatically cast dark shadows throughout the barn, dimming any outside light that had previously made its way through cracks in the wood. There was moisture in the air as well, altering the density inside the barn. The air was heavy, closing in on her. It didn't quite suffocate her, but made it hard to breathe, as if warning her that it could choke her if it wanted to.

Laurie observed the images being displayed. All of the clouds showed pictures of her as an adult. She was picking Royce up from school, going grocery shopping, watching fireworks at a Fourth of July celebration. She remembered those moments, although the timeline was hazy. One thing she did know was that they were nearing present day.

Laurie looked at Royce, hoping for an explanation or a few motivating words. He stared at the mists with a stern expression, as if analyzing them for their content and relevance. He offered no response. She swallowed hard. There was only one thing left to say. Laurie spoke to the open space, as steady as she could manage. "I pray I may, I pray I might, be shown how to heal, thus given new sight."

Thunder reverberated throughout the barn, shaking the columns that supported the balcony above Laurie. The clouds screeched after each other, their voices like daggers piercing the air. Laurie covered her ears, unable to handle the shrill noise. The memories ricocheted off of the barn walls, as if enraged that they had been held captive for so long.

Laurie was starting to question how much longer she could handle the pandemonium when the flames from the fire began licking memories out of the air. Each memory was corralled and roped in, leaving behind no trace of its existence. Into the fire they flew, consumed and digested. Soon, the meal was over, and a calming presence fell over the barn.

Then, one memory was spit back out of the fire and rested in front of them.

The mist expanded like usual, taking Laurie and Royce into its world. Once there, the sound of rain encompassed them. The scene was dark, and for a second, Laurie was unsure if she recalled the memory at all. Colors and images blurred together, slowly melting toward the ground.

Windshield wipers burst across the atmosphere and threw aside water, causing Laurie to jump. They were inside a car. But who was . . . Royce's dad appeared in the driver's seat with an adult Laurie beside him, holding his hand. Both of them laughed playfully.

Laurie left Royce's side and walked forward with her arm outstretched. Silent tears streaked her face as she attempted to reach out and touch her husband on the screen.

His voice vibrated the memory, drawing Laurie's hand back. "How was the food? Did the new restaurant meet the standard?"

"It was absolutely beautiful, babe," Laurie said on the screen. Her smile was radiant. "The flowers, the candles, the venue . . . all of it. Just amazing. I'm a very lucky girl."

"Still not tired of me after twelve years?"

"Still," said Laurie, kissing him on the hand.

In the barn, Laurie ran back to her son. "Please, turn this off. I know what happens, and I can learn, I promise!" She cried out to him in despair. "I can learn. I *have* learned! Just don't show anymore!" She pleaded with her son, but all he did was take her in his arms and hold her close.

Royce was still embracing his mother when a transfer truck ran a red light and plowed into the driver's side door of their family's car. The vehicle spun several times before hitting a telephone pole that stood on the corner of the street. Airbags dangled out of the shattered windows as rain pounded the torn metal. Royce's dad was slumped over the steering wheel while Laurie lay unconscious in the passenger's seat. The car's horn was stuck, blaring loudly. The sound of the horn mixed with the rain faded in the distance as the scene was swished away.

Laurie sank to the ground, weeping. "Please, no more . . . no more . . . please . . ." She swayed back and forth, her sobs of pity breaking each word into syllables. Her body sat hunched in a helpless pile, too fatigued and emotionally tattered to move. Royce sat down beside her and rocked her in his arms. For the next few minutes, the only sounds were the popping of the fire, Laurie's heaving cries, and Royce's soft voice singing in her ear.

"Why?" she demanded suddenly. "Why that scene? Why now?" She shoved Royce's arms aside and crawled away. "I don't need comfort. I need answers. Why do you . . . why does *He* think this is important? There are other ways to learn these lessons."

"Although many ways are good, not all ways are effective. I told you that these last two lessons would be the most difficult to endure—"

"NO!" Laurie screamed. "I'm done playing this game. Why does He think that He can steal everything precious to me? He took everything from me that night!"

She didn't mean to shout at Royce. Like every other thing she had experienced in the barn, she knew that it wasn't his fault. He was simply there to help her. And that was the problem. It was Royce standing before her and not the person who she really needed to scream at. Wasn't that how it had always been? When she needed Him the most, He was nowhere to be found. All He did was use other people to deliver His messages rather than delivering the messages Himself. Royce, Pastor Scoggins, Billy . . . but never *Him*.

"Everything, Mother?" Royce asked. "You think that He took *everything* from you that night? If so, then this lesson is more important than you realize."

"What are you talking about?" Laurie was on the verge of completely losing control. Her jaw was clenched, forcing the tears out of her eyes rather than allowing them to fall naturally. "You say that about every lesson."

"But you have just proven why *this* lesson is so important," Royce said.

"Well then, what is it this time?" Laurie fumed.

Royce's demeanor remained calm and composed. "*You must apply your pain.*"

"Apply?" Laurie repeated, bitterness dripping from her lips. "What does that have to do with me saying that He took everything from me that night?"

"*Everything* implies that you had nothing left . . . but what about me?"

"What about you?"

"While you were lost in your grief, you still had a son waiting for you to embrace him." Royce spoke as if he was an outsider rather than her own son who had lived through the experience.

"That's not what I meant," Laurie started. "It...of course, I had you. I just meant that—"

"No, Mother. He knows your heart, and He knows that when that truck hit your car that night, you died inside. In your mind, you *had* lost everything."

Laurie clenched snow into her fists, as if trying to squeeze the pulp out of her anger. "So is that what His aim is with this lesson? To put more grief on me than I already have? That's wonderful of Him."

Royce continued as if he had not heard her last comment. "To apply something, Mother, constitutes putting it into action, using it for a practical purpose, employing it. It means taking something raw and using it to better your life in some way. When tragedies happen to people, their first response is often to assign the blame and get bitter rather than to apply the pain and get better."

"And how do you expect someone to do that who is hurting? Someone who has lost someone or something that they cherish?" Laurie was clearly confused, but her confusion had defused her anger in hopes of understanding. She tossed aside a handful of snow that she had smashed together with her fist.

"It is a learned skill, something that must be practiced. It is a backward way of thinking that He knows appears crazy to someone who is in pain. But it is relevant nonetheless." Royce scooped up the patch of snow that Laurie had tossed down and began shaping it in his palm as he spoke. "People always ask questions when they are in pain. That's natural, and there is nothing wrong with it. But your healing rests in the motive behind the questions that you ask. When they are at their very worst breaking point, people must develop the ability to ask the right questions."

"Which are?" Laurie asked.

"Typical questions range from 'How is this fair?' to 'Why did I deserve this?' or even your question, 'How could He take everything from me?' They are all understandable and obviously driven by the emotion of the moment. However, the questions that *should* be asked are much more evaluative—'What are you trying to reveal to me through this experience?', 'How can I use this situation to impact other people?', and 'How can I apply these lessons to gain a better perspective on the abundant life you intended me to live?' I know all of these seem robotic, like reading from a script, but the reality is that the heart of the question will determine the healing in the answer.'"

"But I feel like the answers to those questions won't remove the pain," Laurie said. "It seems like they would only breed more questions."

Royce nodded. "The immediate goal is not to remove the pain but to learn how to use the pain to make you a better person. Many people never utilize the lessons they could learn through the things they experience. These things could write a beautiful story of redemption, healing, and hope. They could show the world how to believe in truth again. But too often, people allow their anger and hurt to overshadow everything, and they miss the opportunity that the pain has provided."

"So you are saying to use the pain against itself?" Laurie remarked.

"Yes, that's one way of looking at it. Who do we listen to the most? People who are the least like us or people that are the most like us? If someone has experienced something you have experienced, and they have found peace within it, you would be much more apt to listen to how they came to find that peace over someone who had no way of sympathizing with you but was trying to tell you how to overcome a situation. When you have the ability to recognize the potential that lies within your pain, as well as the maturity to mentor others through the lessons you have learned from your pain, then you will start to see yourself influence others on a much grander scale. But like I said, it is a learned skill."

Laurie's anger, which had been replaced with confusion, was now developing a numbness that she was far too familiar with inside the barn. "So, in this situation, how could I have applied my pain concerning you?"

Royce finished sculpting the snow in his palm. Instead of tossing it back on the ground, he placed it in his jacket pocket. Laurie recognized the gesture but was too engrossed in their conversation to question it further. "When Dad died that night, it left a gaping hole inside of you, but it also left a gaping hole inside of me. You were so confused and broken that you focused more on what you had lost rather than what you still possessed, your own son."

"Royce, I really didn't—"

"No, Mother. This isn't about me, now. I am no longer in pain. I am . . . *new*." He offered his hand to Laurie, and this time, she didn't reject it. "The point of this lesson is not to bring you grief, but to open your eyes to the truth. After the crash, all we had left was each other. You could have used your pain to bring awareness to that fact . . . that it was an opportunity to bring us together and unite us in a way we never had been before. It was a chance to demonstrate to your son how to be brave, how to stand up when life pushes you down, how to rely on each other, how to find the purpose in everything, how to not lose faith, how to not lose hope. But . . ."

"I didn't do that," Laurie finished. Her face loosened, and her shoulders slumped. "I'm so sorry, Royce. You're right. There is so much I could have done differently. So much I *should* have done differently. I'm just . . . so sorry. So very sorry."

Royce smiled sympathetically. "There are still ways to utilize your pain, Mother. For instance, what can you learn from Dad? What did he stand for? What attributes did he possess that you can apply to your own life? What did the incident teach you about your own character? What did it reveal about your core strengths and weaknesses? What did it reveal to you about *His* purpose? All of these are ways to apply your pain in order to make the most of it. Like you said, to use the pain against itself so that the enemy does not triumph through the tragedy."

"But Royce, you talk as if it isn't too late, but . . . Well . . ." She shook her head, unsure of how to finish.

"There is a story yet to be written," said Royce. "There is so much potential that lies within you. By the time we finish here, I think you will have the answers you are looking for. I promise."

Royce helped Laurie to her feet. He was smiling, as he often was. While it helped reassure her that things could get better, she couldn't shake the thought that looming in front of her was one last memory. She took a deep breath and faced the flames.

Chapter 16
The Last Cigarette

An unsettling pain cramped Laurie's stomach, as if her organs were being squeezed together. Her nerves had been destroyed throughout her time in the barn, but this was different. The feeling was sharp and direct.

"The time has come, Mother," Royce said.

The fire flickered, and immediately, a low rumble passed over them. It vibrated the ground beneath them and rattled the balconies on either side of the barn. At first, Laurie thought that it was some type of earthquake tremor, but soon she realized it was thunder. Powerful thunder. And she also realized that there is never thunder without—

A bolt of lightning coursed through the air, splintering off in all directions. Laurie grabbed Royce, her fear replaced with terror. Another bolt shot through the barn, striking the rafters and falling away. More thunder followed it, making Laurie's knees weak. She clutched Royce tighter, anticipating the next strike. Seconds later, a streak of lightning lit up the entire atmosphere, like one gigantic, prolonged picture flash. Laurie screamed. The mists had shown signs of storm clouds, but now, the storm had actually arrived.

Royce put his arm around Laurie, offering her the strength she badly needed to endure the last challenge. He had to speak loud to be heard over the lightning and thunder. "This is the last lesson, Mother. You have seen that there are things in life that are beyond your control, and that learning to accept that is an integral part of being at peace with your past. You have seen that forgiving others is not about what it does *for* them but what it does *in* you; that surrendering your pain allows Him to remove your burdens because they are no longer yours to carry. You have seen how forgiving yourself forces you to focus on His unconditional grace, which gives you the strength to release the pain that binds you. And you have just seen how applying your pain enables you to learn from it, utilize it, and maximize its effectiveness in your pursuit of an abundant life. Now, you will be shown the fifth and most important lesson on your journey to healing. It is the most vital step, for without it, the other four have no meaning and serve no real purpose." Royce nodded at her. "When you are ready, Mother."

Laurie cast a fearful glance at the lightning, then at the white flames of the fire, then back at her son. With teeth chattering, she fumbled through the prayer that she had learned all too well. "I p-pray I may, I pray I might, b-be shown how to heal, thus given . . . thus given new sight."

The fire went out.

The white flames dissolved into themselves. There was no leftover residue of black ashes, no burned surface, no trace that any fire had ever existed. Snow covered the ground just as it did the rest of the barn floor. They were left in complete darkness, other than the occasional flash of lightning to offer them vision. Laurie once again felt the ground rumbling beneath her. This time, however, it wasn't thunder.

Where the fire had just burned, a block of stone began rising out of the ground. She only caught glimpses of it, visible when the lightning would strike, but she recognized the object immediately. She had traced its outline too many times to forget one inch of it. The top emerged, followed by the inscription, and finally, the base. A small square stone with rounded corners.

Laurie forgot about the lightning around her and the snow beneath her and the fear inside her. Everything was suddenly small and insignificant compared to the stone.

She approached it slowly, reverently. With each burst of lightning, the letters grew more distinct.

Royce Chandler Vickers
October 25, 2006–April 24, 2017

"He danced when the clouds were dark,
sang when the storm was loud, and loved when others lost sight.
This love will always be remembered."

The fact that her son was standing right behind her, in whatever form he existed, faded from her conscious mind. The Royce that she had known, the Royce that she had let *die*, was directly in front of her. It was the final wound that had driven her to this place, but even in The World of White, she was not able to outrun it.

Laurie knelt to the ground as she had done so many times in the graveyard back home. She stretched out her hand and slowly traced the outline of each figure. Letter after letter, number after number—her finger pressed into the stone progressively harder. Her tears fell silently, blinding her eyes. She did nothing to stop the stinging sensation. The same familiar, paralyzing pain that she had always felt resurfaced at the feel of the concrete indentions beneath her fingertip. She was in a barn, in another dimension, yet she was in the same place she had always been. Her emotions finally broke, and she lunged forward, embracing the tombstone with all of her strength.

As she did, the atmosphere began to shift. The thunder hushed, and the lightning quit shrieking. Images appeared on the inside of the barn. They were dim, but they were much brighter than the dark setting of the storm that had just swept through. Laurie looked up from Royce's grave and scanned the barn, trying to grasp the scene in its totality. They were in the living room of her apartment. Royce had his backpack on and was preparing to walk out of the house. He turned to his mother, who was lying on the couch. "I have a ride home today, so don't worry about picking me up. My friend said that he can give me a ride home whenever I need it. Love you!" He offered a cheerful smile and opened the door. On the couch, Laurie shielded her eyes from the light that streamed inside and gave a faint nod.

As Laurie sat in front of the tombstone watching herself, panic spread over her body. She began shaking violently. She had known that there was no friend. She remembered lying on the sofa, aware of that fact, and had still allowed her son to walk out the door. She hadn't bothered to apologize, to tell him that she loved him, or to offer to help him get home. She had simply let him leave. She had let him walk out of her life. This scene wasn't just another normal school day, even though many had passed just like it. This day was different. It was *the* day. The last day she had seen Royce alive.

Images flashed across the barn, highlighting Royce's final day. He was walking into school, turning in his homework, eating lunch in the school's cafeteria, laughing with his friends during a group activity, swinging on the playground, and finally, bounding down the steps when school let out.

Laurie stood without realizing she was standing. Using the tombstone to support her, she slowly rotated in a complete circle, enamored with the images that flashed around her. She had never known the details of that day. How Royce looked, how he felt, what his last moments were like. If he was happy or sad or scared. That was part of what made that day so difficult . . . not knowing. Now, she would see it all for the first time.

The scene rolled forward.

Royce walked out of Bradburn's Grocery holding three packs of Horseshoe Maverick candy cigarettes. He put two of the packs in his backpack and took the wrapper off of the third. Laurie watched the memory with remorse. The sight of her son alive was beautiful as well as painful. Royce had always claimed he was a "chain-smoker eater." One day, he had shown her how he "smoked" his candy cigarettes. She recalled each step in her mind, still amused at how well he could mimic it.

Her thoughts seemed to be creating the images in front of her as the clips in the scene shadowed the memories she was envisioning. Royce thumped the pack of cigarettes in his hand until one slid out. Sticking it in his mouth, he reached into his back pocket and formed an imaginary lighter with his fist and thumb. He paused momentarily to wave at a passing car, then returned his attention to the task at hand. He cupped his left hand over the cigarette to block the wind, and after flicking his thumb a few times to get the lighter going, lit the end of the butt.

Royce looked to the sky and took a long, slow drag. Then, he grabbed the cigarette between his pointer and middle finger and took it away. He blew into the wind, laughing. It would have almost been comical if not for the inevitable fate of the memory. He checked to see if any cars were coming, crossed the street, and strolled down the sidewalk humming cheerfully. It was a happy scene. A content scene. At any moment, it might have seemed that trouble was miles away, but Laurie knew better.

Royce was passing the post office when a loud cry jerked his head around. He slowed his walk and gazed in the direction of the noise. The scene panned around to show what he was looking at. Behind the post office, shadows crisscrossed back and forth on the ground. They rose and fell, tussling with each other. Royce took another drag on his cigarette, bit off the end, and began munching it as he inched along the side of the building.

Laurie could not restrain herself. She ran to one of the beams that supported the balcony and folded around it. She knew that there was no way to change what happened next, that Royce had already died and was no longer in pain, yet it didn't stop her from trying to prevent it from happening. She watched the scene unfold above her and screamed at the walls of the barn. She begged Royce to ignore what he had heard and to turn around and go home, but he didn't. Of course, he didn't. His character hadn't allowed him. He was too brave for that.

The shadows grew larger as Royce approached them. He carefully peeked around the corner of the building. A young black kid was getting beaten up by two older boys. The older boys looked like they were in their late middle school or early high school years, but Laurie wasn't sure. The kid they were bullying had a cut eyebrow, and every item from his backpack was strewn across the ground. Each time he tried to stand up, the older boys shoved him back down, laughing.

Understanding dawned in Laurie's eyes. Royce's journal. She remembered the entry he had written about a boy getting beaten up on the abandoned ball field near their house. Royce mentioned how afraid he had been and how he had run away when the bully caught him staring. It all made sense now. She could see it in her son's eyes on the screen. Royce wasn't just defending someone who couldn't defend himself, he was righting a wrong. He was refusing to let fear win again. He was redeeming himself.

Royce walked out into the open.

With a quick jolt, he sprinted toward the group and hurled himself into one of the older boys. He hit the boy so hard that the impact knocked the candy cigarette out of Royce's own mouth. The older boy toppled over, more surprised than injured. His friend shot around to see who had shoved him. He dropped the kid with the cut eyebrow and stepped toward Royce.

"Now, who do we have here?" He turned to the small kid on the ground and threw his thumb back at Royce. "You know him? Your little friend coming to save you?" Neither Royce nor the kid spoke a word. The boy turned back to Royce. "Well, isn't that cute. Trying to be a hero. You should have just kept to yourself. Guess you'll have to join him now."

Royce threw his hands up to defend himself, but it was no use against the older boy's strength. He slung Royce against the wall of the building. Royce collapsed to his knees, the wind clearly knocked out of him. Laurie fell to her knees as well, still gripping the balcony post. While Royce gasped for air on the screen, Laurie gasped for air in the barn. Both of their bodies heaved in unison.

"Stop! Please!" the younger kid cried. Still taking long, deep breaths, Royce reached over and touched the kid's arm. It looked like he was trying to comfort him and reassure him that everything would be okay.

Using the wall as leverage, Royce hoisted himself slowly back to his feet. He looked at the kid on the ground and said, "It's okay. They can't hurt you unless you let them. Not really hurt you, anyway. These are just their masks. They're just trying to find their *blue*."

The boys raised their eyebrows in confusion, sneered, and rushed at Royce. Laurie's screams echoed throughout the barn as her son was hit again, and again, and again. The sound of each blow tore a new gash in her soul, while the sound of Royce struggling singed that gash with a hot iron.

Royce lay crumpled on the ground, still conscious, but badly bruised. The older boy that he had shoved picked Royce up by the shoulders and forced him to stand. Struggling to maintain his balance, Royce had to lean against the wall for support. The boy pointed a finger in Royce's face. "Don't ever, *ever*, get in our way again. Take your little charcoal friend and get out of here." Both older boys began walking away.

Laurie looked up. Somewhere inside of her, beyond the sleepless nights and the hungover mornings, past the endless days at the graveyard and the countless hours screaming at the walls, something sparked. Hope. The boys were walking away. They were leaving Royce alone. Maybe they hadn't killed him. Maybe the last few months had been one, long, horrifying nightmare. Maybe Royce really was alive and she would wake up to find him back in his bed.

But then . . .

On the screen, Royce said something. It was low and strained, but it was enough to make one of the boys turn around. Horror spread over Laurie's face as any notion of hope that her boy was still alive, faded. The boy walked back to Royce and faced him again. "What did you say?"

Royce gulped, trying to get the energy to speak. Finally, he opened his mouth again, his voice hushed. "I forgive you," he whispered.

The boy's eyes flushed in rage. He looked back at his friend, shaking his head in disbelief. Then, in one quick movement, he shoved his arm into Royce's stomach. He paused there for a moment, then stepped back cautiously. A black marble handle was sticking out of Royce's shirt. Everyone on the screen fell silent. In the barn, Laurie shrieked and grabbed her side, as if the knife had impaled her as well.

Royce looked down at the object, his face expressionless. He wrapped both hands around the handle and pulled out the silver blade. Rays of sun gleamed off the red liquid dripping from its tip. The knife slipped from his grasp as his body eased down the wall toward the ground. Both older boys sprinted away.

The small kid rushed over to Royce and pulled Royce's head into his lap. He looked around and began crying for help, but no one heard him. He held Royce close and patted his cheek and pleaded with him not to die.

Seconds later, Royce exhaled for the last time, and his body went limp.

A gust of wind blew, sending his candy cigarette tumbling away.

Just as the small boy had coddled Royce, Laurie allowed her son to coddle her. The tombstone sank into the ground, and the white campfire returned. Laurie's sobs were deep and hoarse, emitting from every part of her trembling body.

"I'm so sorry," she whimpered. "So . . . so . . . sorry. My precious boy . . . I'm so sorry." All she could do was repeat that phrase, over and over again as Royce rocked her in his arms. For the next few minutes, Royce stroked his mother's hair, kissed her on the cheek, and whispered in her ear that everything was all right.

When her cries grew silent, Royce gently pulled Laurie back so that he could see her face. "It's okay now, Mother. The pain is gone. Look." He spread apart his jacket and lifted his shirt. Instead of a small scar below his abdomen, his skin was smooth and wholesome. "It's like new," Royce said, smiling.

"I don't understand," Laurie said, tears still staining her words. The emotions of the last five scenes from her past had culminated to leave her completely drained of energy. "Did He want me to have peace knowing what really happened that day? Is that why He wanted me to see it?" She continued to wipe tears from her eyes as Royce responded.

"He knew that it would give you a sense of closure to know what happened that day, but no, that was not His ultimate purpose in showing you that clip. His purpose is far greater. It is the doorway to the final lesson. It brings together everything you have seen and heard so far. Most importantly, it will perhaps offer the greatest explanation as to why you are here and what all of this means."

"Then, what is the lesson?" Laurie asked.

Royce's eyes shone. "Follow me, and I'll show you, Mother."

Chapter 17
A Butterfly's Wings

R oyce marched toward the barn entrance with Laurie close
behind him. He reached for the doors and pried them open
as he had done when they first arrived. Light exploded into
the barn, forcefully overtaking them. Laurie blocked her face with
her forearm, the clarity of the outer world temporarily blinding her.

Once outside, Royce shut the doors behind them. Laurie opened
and closed her eyes several times, blinking away the spots that danced
in her vision. She wasn't sure how long they had been in the barn,
but everything outside was just as they had left it. The valley below
them with the lake and the weeping willow, the endless row of hills
beyond the valley, the tone of the sky, and the white world surrounding them—all pure and majestic and undefiled. Laurie squinted her
eyes as they continued to adjust to the new terrain.

"This way, Mother." Royce walked away from the barn and
trudged down the hill that led into the valley. Laurie followed in his
tracks, once again picking up her dress in order to walk unimpeded.
She watched her bare feet dip into the snow and emerge out of it,
step after step after step. She fell into a rhythmic trance, the scenes
from the barn replaying in her mind. What was she supposed to do
with the memories she had seen and the lessons that had been reinforced? Did Royce really expect her to immediately grasp each of the
concepts he had introduced? He spoke as if her journey to discovery
had just started, while she knew that her life had just ended. How
was she supposed to even begin processing everything?

As the ground leveled out, Royce led them around the lake, to the base of the willow tree. They stood underneath the protection of its branches, looking out over the calm, still waters. The lake looked at peace, as if nothing had ever disturbed it. Laurie felt that it had its own soul and its own heartbeat and its own sense of purpose. She felt safe, at rest.

"This is where the journey ends," said Royce, looking across the lake. "This is where the final lesson waits."

Laurie acknowledged his comment, even though she didn't know what she was supposed to be seeing. There was no fire, no mists, no thunder or lightning. The lake showed no signs of life at all. Either way, she knew how the process worked. She turned to face the lake and said, "I pray I may, I pray I might—"

"Actually, Mother," Royce said, smiling. "Now, it's my turn."

Royce placed his hand on the trunk of the willow and closed his eyes. Laurie didn't know whether she was supposed to close her eyes or not, but she kept her gaze locked on her son. He looked as if he was no longer with her. As if his body had left and only his spirit remained. Then, he opened his mouth and prayed.

"I pray you may, bestow unto me, the power to reveal a future destiny."

A massive *thud* shook the ground, as if a meteor had landed next to them. Laurie's knees went limp. She grabbed Royce to maintain her balance as the shock sent ripples echoing across the water in front of them. A gust of wind swept over the weeping willow, contorting its branches in all directions. For a few seconds, the tree enveloped them like a blanket, hiding the sky above them. Laurie wondered if it would stay like that forever, but the branches soon retreated, and the serene atmosphere returned. The water had just grown completely still when four limbs from the weeping willow began lowering again. There was no wind or earth tremor to send them into motion this time. They moved on their own, stretching mechanically toward the surface of the water. Each of their tips dipped softly into the lake. Laurie thought they looked like children sticking their toes in the pool to test the temperature of the water. She imagined Mother Willow behind them, urging her kids to quit stalling and dive in. When the four branches emerged from the water, four images rose with them. Connected to the tip of each branch was a metallic hologram of a child. They all appeared roughly the same age as Royce. Their faces looked familiar, but Laurie was having trouble placing them.

Each hologram played forward as if it were a live video feed. The first image displayed a Chinese boy lying on his stomach drawing symbols in a notebook. He was smiling and kicking his feet in the air, obviously enjoying the activity. The second image showed a Mexican girl playing on a swing set in her backyard. Her ponytail swung side to side as she went from the swing to the slide to the monkey bars. The third image presented an Arab boy praying with his family at their dinner table. Even though his head was bowed, he kept peeping around the table every few seconds to see what everyone was doing. The last image revealed an African American boy sitting on the side of the road eating an apple. He was munching the fruit contently and waving at cars that passed by. The branches floated away, leaving the holograms hovering on the surface of the water.

"Each of these images holds the key to the fifth lesson," said Royce. Laurie had almost forgotten that he was standing there. "In case you are wondering, yes, you are already familiar with their stories. They are each connected to my former life in a way that only you can understand at the moment."

Royce's subtle reference unlocked her memories. She remembered these children. She had read about them in Royce's journal. They were the kids that Royce had reached out to. The ones who no one else wanted to befriend. The ones who had a voice but needed help finding it. The ones who ultimately had brought more pain into Royce's life. And in the case of the last hologram, the one who had led to Royce's death. They were at Royce's funeral as well, though at the time, they were no more meaningful to Laurie than anyone else who had attended. They had all been an echo in the backdrop of her pain. But now, now that things were piecing together, Laurie could finally understand their significance.

She turned to her son. "How do they teach a lesson about overcoming my pain? They were obviously a part of your life, not mine. How are they a part of the fifth lesson of my healing?"

Royce's face beamed. "You will see shortly, Mother. This is the moment that you have been waiting for, even though you have never realized it." He pointed at the holograms. "Their stories will provide a better explanation for how to deal with your pain than perhaps any lesson you have experienced so far."

"But how?" Laurie asked. "How will that happen?"

Royce replied, "By showing you a world that does not yet exist."

Laurie's face crinkled in confusion. At this point, she no longer bothered trying to disguise her skepticism.

Royce was too excited to slow down. "The one who has made this entire journey possible has granted me a special gift. He has allowed me to take you into the future! We will show you not only who these children will become, but also how their stories will impact the world around them. *That* is where you will learn the final lesson."

Royce's face shone with a color that she had not seen since she had arrived in The World of White. After Royce showed her the first memory from her childhood, she never imagined that she would make it to this point. She couldn't fathom that she would have the mental or emotional energy to still be breathing. And in some regards, she was right. She was completely depleted. But Royce's passion had sparked a new feeling in her. It contained a new sense of curiosity. A new sense of anticipation. Was she finally getting answers?

Royce faced the holograms. "Show us."

All four images descended into the water. Immediately, the placid surface began to morph, the once white reflection now bursting with colors and pictures and motion. A new set of holograms grew out of the lake illustrating the Chinese boy and his family. The 3D scene stretched across the entire surface, lapping onto every shore. As the pictures rolled forward, Royce began narrating.

"His name is Kim. When I met him, his family had just moved from a small city in China. He was having a difficult time adjusting to a new culture and a new home, as any kid would in his situation. He tried to curb his discouragement by focusing on his studies and the other responsibilities that his parents required of him. They had paid for private tutors to teach him how to play the piano, how to speak Korean, and how to use proper swimming techniques in order to keep a balanced exercise routine. His parents were not blind to his discomfort. They recognized his struggle and grew increasingly worried about him."

As Royce spoke, the holograms on the lake displayed the various scenes that he described: *Kim getting pushed aside in the hallway, spilling his books. Kim's trainer correcting his form and making him swim another lap. Kim sitting quietly at the dinner table while his parents looked at him sympathetically.*

"Unbeknownst to Kim, his parents were also having a difficult time adjusting. His father's business partner had moved back to China for a family emergency, temporarily leaving the fate of the business to Kim's mother and father. The weight of their responsibilities, along with the strain of adjusting to their new lifestyle as a family, caused stress that they had not anticipated. Two weeks before I met Kim, they had decided that if things did not improve, they would be forced to move back to China." *Kim's father slamming the phone down at work, frustrated. Kim's parents arguing quietly in the next room while Kim lay on the floor of his bedroom doing homework. Kim's mother working late into the night, balancing financial books and typing invoices.*

"Then, I helped Kim pick up his books at school. From that day forward, our friendship began to develop. Kim returned from school every day with a little more vigor and a new sense of encouragement." *Kim and Royce walking down the hallway together, chatting excitedly. Kim completing his piano lessons with a positive attitude.* "Witnessing Kim's transformation gave his parents the extra bit of inspiration they needed to press forward. Life was in no way easy, but they made it work, and soon, their business began turning a profit. They decided against the move and chose to remain in the United States." *Kim's dad returning home early from work. Kim laughing with his parents while they walked through their neighborhood together.*

As Royce finished his last sentence, all the holograms of Kim's family dissolved. Laurie was still confused. She didn't understand how Royce's compassion toward people would help her overcome her pain. It sounded selfish, but wasn't that the whole point?

To show her how to heal?

"Now, for the second story," Royce said, interrupting her thoughts. Laurie refocused her attention. A new set of holograms rose from the surface of the water, this time displaying the young Mexican girl with dark hair flowing down her back. Just like the story of Kim, images created themselves as Royce spoke them into existence.

"This is Luciana," Royce began. "Luciana's father moved their family to the United States because her mother had cancer and needed access to better treatment. It was a very difficult time mentally and emotionally for Luciana's entire family. Luciana took things especially hard. She began losing her appetite and secluding herself from social interaction. At school, it was difficult to make friends, and she grew even more introverted with each passing day." *Luciana playing with a doll by herself in her living room. Luciana sitting quietly at her desk while other students answered the teacher's questions. Luciana standing by the playground fence watching a group of girls laughing together.*

"Then, the day arrived when I asked her to play with me on the swing set. Although she was still upset about her mother's condition, the new friendship gave her an outlet to express her feelings and find happiness again. I introduced her to Kim, and all three of us formed a beautiful friendship." *Luciana smiling on a swing, her head tilted back and her hair sweeping the ground. Royce, Luciana, and Kim eating together in the cafeteria, laughing as they each tried to make faces with their food.*

"Luciana asked her father to build a swing set behind their house so that she could play whenever she liked. While swinging a few weeks later, she saw her neighbor across the street sitting alone, watching her. Luciana asked the girl if she wanted to come over and join her, and the girl reluctantly agreed. Neither of them had any idea that they would soon be best friends." *Luciana chasing a blonde-haired girl down the slide in her backyard. The two girls having a stuffed animal tea party in Luciana's room. The two girls rollerblading around a cul-de-sac in their neighborhood.*

"But how amazing is this?" Royce continued, "Luciana found out that the girl's father is a doctor who specializes in rare forms of cancer. Even though Luciana's family could not afford the treatments, he worked it out to get Luciana's mother the help that she needed. Her cancer is now in remission." *The two families grilling out together. Luciana's mother sitting in a hospital room crying tears of joy as the doctor showed her how the new treatments were curing her cancer.*

The holograms once again disappeared into the lake, only to be replaced with a third set. Royce began addressing them before Laurie had a chance to ask any questions.

"The third story is particularly intriguing. The boy's name is Rasheed. His family had to relocate when civil war broke out in their home country of Saudi Arabia. Since they are Muslims, their transition to the United States was in many ways more difficult than other foreigners entering the country. They were met with much skepticism and resentment." *Rasheed's family kneeling on prayer mats one morning. Kids whispering to each other and pointing at Rasheed as he passed them on the street. People staring at Rasheed's mother distastefully in a department store as she scolded Rasheed's little sister for not wearing her hijab correctly.* "But this story is actually not about Rasheed. It's about Rasheed's older brother, Ahmed. You see, Ahmed was just entering high school, and he was having a particularly difficult time adjusting to his environment. He had secretly grown suicidal, exhausted by the racism and hatred that he received from his American classmates." *Ahmed opening notes in his locker with curse words and racial slurs written on them. Ahmed ducking his head out of embarrassment while his family walked into their mosque to worship. Ahmed crying in his bedroom, shaking his head violently and pounding his bed.*

"The day that I helped Rasheed in the street, Ahmed had come home from school planning to commit suicide when his family went to sleep that night. But when he heard Rasheed share the story of the American boy who had befriended him, something changed inside Ahmed. It was only a tiny spark of hope, but it was all he needed. It was the notion that not all people were bad. That there was a source of goodness in the world." *Ahmed sitting on the stairs listening to Rasheed tell his story in the kitchen. Ahmed journaling his thoughts that night after everyone else had gone to bed.* "He reluctantly decided to hold off on his plans to end his life. As days turned into weeks, Ahmed recovered further and developed methods to cope with his surroundings. Within a few months, he had made peace with himself and others, and thus found happiness." *Ahmed ignoring insults from fellow classmates and continuing to walk down the hall. Ahmed laughing with his siblings while playing board games with them.*

Royce finished his story as all of the holograms collapsed into the lake. Before he could start another string of events, Laurie interjected. "Royce, wait. I'm sorry, but I'm still having trouble putting everything together. You insisted that this would provide an explanation, but what does any of this have to do with my healing? Your heart was so humble, so forgiving, so compassionate. I see that. I know that you cared for people and loved people and sacrificed for them. But it looks like that this should offer *you* peace, not me. What is the purpose of it all?"

Royce acknowledged his mother's question by taking her hand and kissing it.

"The purpose of it all lies in what you *haven't* seen, Mother."

"Please," Laurie said dejected, "just tell me what you mean."

"It's called the chaos theory," said Royce.

"The chaos theory," repeated Laurie.

"Essentially, it is a mathematical theory that states that the slightest change in conditions can alter the outcomes of a system beyond anything that human beings can measure or predict. I know it sounds complicated, but don't dismiss it just yet," Royce said as Laurie opened her mouth to protest. "Over time, the theory would come to be known by a different name—the butterfly effect. It simplifies the theory by saying that the flap of a butterfly's wings on one side of the earth can create a tsunami on the other side of the earth. It is an extremely intriguing concept, Mother."

"Royce, I—"

"I know it seems disorienting, but don't worry. I'll explain it," he reassured her. "If you apply this logic, then you will see that every decision you make, no matter how small or seemingly insignificant, can create a chain of events that influences mankind in a way that is beyond all levels of comprehension. Every choice you make and every choice you choose *not* to make has consequences. Those can be positive or negative. No detail of life is insignificant."

Royce walked to the edge of the lake and tapped his foot in the water. Small ripples echoed across the surface, stretching farther and farther into the distance. "One small tap, Mother, can ripple into the future in ways you cannot foresee. Or to take it a step further, one minor decision can impact the life of a child that has not yet been born. *He* controls the tides of the universe, but He has given *us* the freedom to choose where and how we step into the water."

Royce returned to his mother's side. "You have just seen how He used my life to impact those around me. Now, He wants to show you how He will intertwine each of those lives to impact the future of the world. It may seem a little complex, even a little farfetched, but you must believe in what you are about to see. It will show you how all of the pieces fit together. Are you ready, Mother?"

Laurie nodded without speaking, and together, they turned their attention back to the lake.

"Show us," Royce said once more. The same intense *thud* punched the foundation beneath them, sending shimmers across the lake and the white hills beyond it. A new set of holograms sprouted from the surface of the water. A determined grin spread across Royce's face, and he began talking.

"Since they have chosen to remain in the United States, Kim will eventually earn his citizenship and graduate from high school with honors." *Kim walking across the stage of his high school, shaking his principal's hand.* "He will end up falling in love with a girl at the college he will attend, and they will get married his senior year." *Kim proposing on one knee under a candlelit gazebo. Kim and his wife releasing Chinese lanterns into the sky at their wedding reception.* "On their third wedding anniversary, they will find out that Kim's wife is pregnant with a little boy. That boy will go on to become the future president of the United States." *Kim holding his newborn son for the first time in a hospital. Kim and his wife at a campaign rally to support their son. Kim's son standing on the steps of the Capitol, being sworn in as president.*

"This is where things start to grow more intricate," Royce pressed on. "What the world doesn't know yet is that a corrupt sect will rise in the Saudi Arabian government that will attempt to overthrow their King, threaten to enslave the nation, and potentially commit terrorist acts that would have global ramifications. But Kim's son and the United States will intervene. Working with the king of Saudi Arabia and his trusted foreign advisors, Kim's son and the US government will help stabilize the situation in Saudi Arabia, thus preventing thousands of deaths from occurring." *Saudi men dressed completely in black making terrorist demands on live television. Kim's son shaking hands with foreign leaders as people around them cheer. Articles on the front page of U.S. newspapers declaring peace in the Middle East.*

The holograms vanished. "We will come back to Luciana," Royce said. "First, let's take a look at Ahmed, Rasheed's brother." A new set of holograms appeared, and without any delay, Royce began discussing them.

"Ahmed will go on to get a bachelor's degree in business and a master's degree in international affairs. He will become engrossed with the idea that peace *can* exist in the Middle East and will move back to his home in Saudi Arabia shortly after graduating." *Ahmed holding his master's diploma and taking pictures with his family. Ahmed's family throwing a going away party in preparation for his move back to Saudi Arabia.* "Ahmed will spend years working his way into the political scene and will be elected to various prominent political positions. While in office, he will meet a lovely woman, and they will get married two years later." *Ahmed waving to a crowd of supporters after winning an election. Ahmed and his wife moving into their first home together.* "Ahmed and his wife will also have a child. Ahmed will instill in his son the importance of national pride, political stability, and global peace. When he grows older, Ahmed's son will follow in his father's footsteps and also pursue a political career. Ahmed's son will be loved by his people, and after much patience and hard work, he will eventually be appointed the personal advisor to the king of Saudi Arabia." *Ahmed's son sitting in the front row watching his dad deliver a speech. Ahmed hugging his son as his son is elected to his first political position. Ahmed's son bowing reverently to the king as the king enters the room.*

"But here is the most captivating aspect of his story," Royce said. "When the corrupt sect rises in the Saudi Arabian government,

Ahmed's son will be the leader of the diplomatic team who will help advise the king in his interactions with the United States. Ahmed's son will also assist the king in establishing a firm relationship with Kim's son, the president of the United States. Together, the team will work to eradicate corruption within the Saudi Arabian government and ensure peace to its people." *Ahmed's son making propositions to the king of Saudi Arabia. Ahmed's son drinking coffee with Kim's son. People celebrating in the streets of various Saudi Arabian cities over the end of corruption.*

Royce paused to make sure that Laurie was still with him. She was still focused intently on the water—quiet, but composed. "Now, back to Luciana," he said. The holograms returned.

"Once Luciana's mother is completely cured of cancer, she will attend a university in the United States to further her education. She will enter into the medical field and begin studying cures for rare forms of cancer like her own." *Luciana's mother taking notes in class. Luciana's mother in a science lab dropping liquid into test tubes.* "Her mother's hard work and dedication will inspire Luciana, and she will go on to graduate college with the same degree as her mother. They will eventually move back to Mexico and start their own organization. It will specialize in providing medical care specifically for underprivileged families with cancer needs." *Luciana and her mother standing in front of a new building, cutting a ribbon together for its grand opening. Luciana and her mother working side by side to administer help to a young girl receiving chemotherapy treatments.*

"After her mother passes away, Luciana will run the organization and work to expand her mother's dream. Years later, their organization will provide medical aid to a boy named Ángel Valentin. He will have the same rare form of cancer that Luciana's mother had, but due to the help he receives from their clinic, he will be cured from the disease." *Luciana hanging a picture of her mother in the lobby of their building to honor her memory. Luciana leading staff meetings in a conference room. Ángel hugging Luciana to thank her for saving his life.* "Ángel will grow older and eventually work for a special police task force in Mexico City. During an undercover raid of a powerful drug cartel, he will discover plans they made to orchestrate an assassination attempt on the president of the United States, Kim's son. Ángel will foil the plan, thus protecting a national tragedy from occurring." *Ángel kicking in a door of an abandoned warehouse and storming inside the building with his team. Ángel talking on the phone with the director of the CIA, discussing information found on a hard drive retrieved from one of the cartel's informants.*

When the last hologram of Ángel fell into the lake, Royce turned to his mother. "I know that was a lot to digest, but I imagine that you are starting to sense how all of this is connected. Before we move on and discuss this lesson on a deeper level, however, I have a fourth story to show you—the story of the African American boy. I purposefully saved it for last because I think it has a beautiful way of encompassing the heart of the butterfly effect. Its impact will not be seen on as grand a scale as the other three stories, but it will be no less influential. The journey is almost finished, Mother. Thank you for having the courage to venture this far. Now, for the last story."

As the fourth set of holograms rose from the lake, Royce smiled at them as if he was being reunited with a long lost friend.

"I love each of the people that I have showed you," Royce said. "Their friendships genuinely birthed some of the happiest moments of my life. But this last story is unique in its own way. His name is Jarel. The day I rescued him wasn't the first time that he had been bullied, but it *was* the first time that anyone had ever stood in the gap and taken his place. After he watched me die in his lap, his life would never be the same. You see, with each of the other cases, I entered their lives when they needed support the most—Kim with his parents, Luciana with her mother, Rasheed with his brother. The impact I had on each of their lives will directly influence the lives of their families. That single event in Jarel's life, however, will directly impact him *personally*. Just as I sacrificed myself to save him physically, he will sacrifice himself to save the world spiritually. I'll show you what I mean." The holograms began shifting again as Royce talked. His voice was eager, and his words burst with excitement.

"Jarel will go on to graduate from college with a degree in creative writing. Inspired by my story, he will write a series of novels that chronicle the life of a boy who is determined to eradicate social and racial inequality from the world. The first book in the series will eventually become a best-seller, propelling Jarel to national stardom." *Jarel accepting an award at his university for a short story that he wrote. Jarel drinking coffee in a café while brainstorming ideas for his books. Jarel taking pictures with eager fans at his first book signing.* "That will only be the start of Jarel's journey. Motivated by his vision to see lives transformed, he will decide to use his talent for writing as a platform to reinvest into people's futures. His ministry will use the proceeds that he earns from each book to fund local and global humanitarian projects.

"His first novel will be used to start an organization that rescues women who have been involved in sex trafficking and help them adapt back into society. The organization will become so prominent that when Kim's son becomes president of the United States, he will start a global initiative to fund the program. Millions of women across the world will be given the opportunity to start a new life." *Kim's son proposing a bill to his cabinet to fund the organization. Police handcuffing men on the ground while wrapping blankets around bruised women and leading them to shelter. Young women embracing their counselors in gratitude as they are provided housing and taught basic life skills.*

"Jarel's second novel will be used to provide education for impoverished villages in Saudi Arabia where terrorist and gang activity have ruined their social infrastructure. Schools will be rebuilt, teachers will be hired, and supplies will be distributed. It will take years, along with the help of many government employees and volunteers, but the school systems will eventually regain their strength, establish their identity, and help thousands of kids earn their diploma. One of those kids will be Ahmed's son. The leadership and guidance he will receive throughout his adolescent years will equip him with the skills he will need to be successful as an adult." *Construction workers pouring concrete slabs and stacking bricks into place. Saudi children singing as they carry new desks into their classroom that just arrived on a delivery truck. Ahmed's son showing his parents a project he completed at school.*

"Jarel's third novel will be used to support the organization that Luciana and her mother founded together. The money will allow them to advance their technology, build a new wing for their facility, and travel to remote locations in Mexico to rescue children who would have otherwise died from their illnesses. These innovations will be directly responsible for Ángel's treatment and recovery." *Luciana picking up dirt with a shovel to break ground on the new wing of the building. Luciana's team traveling through mountain passes to offer aid to families in need. Ángel smiling and waving goodbye as he leaves Luciana's clinic for the last time.*

The holograms of Jarel finally evaporated. "So many lives will be redeemed, Mother. Orphanages will be built, fresh water wells will be dug, drug smugglers will be removed from the streets, child armies will be disbanded, starving families will be given healthy food to eat. By taking his passion and reinvesting it, Jarel will help bring hope to the hopeless and life to the lifeless. He will help mend the broken and free the enslaved—one ripple at a time."

Royce turned to face Laurie and took both of her hands in his own. "I know that you never expected to be on this journey. You had no idea that you would wake up in a world where you would experience the very pain you sought to leave behind. It has been tormenting and relentless. But do you want to know why He has allowed me to show you these things, Mother? Why He gave you the strength to endure to this very moment? It's because . . ." Royce's words caught in his throat. Laurie looked up. For the first time since she had arrived in The World of White, she saw tears glistening in the corners of his eyes. He didn't speak. He *couldn't* speak. He simply squeezed her hands and swallowed his cries as his emotions swept over him. It lasted for a second. It lasted for eternity. Finally, he found his voice again. "It's because He is sovereign. *God* is sovereign. That's what all of this has been about—the barn and the fire and the memories and the tears. It all hinges upon this final lesson . . .*You must believe in the sovereignty of God.*"

Laurie looked away, now overcome by her own emotions. So many parts of her body ached from crying—her head, her eyes, her throat, her muscles. She had exhausted that resource as an outlet for her pain. There comes a point where there is nothing left to think, nothing left to say, nothing left to feel. She only *thought* that she had reached that point earlier, but now, she had officially arrived.

Silence seemed to be the only answer. All she could do was shake her head and ponder the thoughts that wouldn't surface, the words that wouldn't form, and the emotions that wouldn't materialize.

"I know that's not what you were hoping to hear," Royce said. "but the reality is that it cannot be denied. We will never be able to make sense of everything created because we were never created to make sense of everything. We are merely human. We have a limited view of life and eternity, and there is no way for us to fully comprehend the story of the world. Like Pastor Scoggins told you not too long ago, only the author of the story adequately understands his creation, his purpose, and his plan."

Laurie couldn't muster the strength to look her son in the eyes. Pastor Scoggins had tried to communicate the same things to her when she had visited him at church, and she hadn't listened then. She didn't want to listen now either, but she had no choice. Laurie knew it was the truth, no matter how unfair or how illogical or how much she hated to admit it. She had always known it. If you took all of her problems and stripped them to their core, her underlying issue with each of them would be the same: God's sovereignty. She had blocked it from her mind, cursed it, and refused to believe in it. She needed justification. She needed someone to blame. She needed the world to make sense. But now, the time for running was over. She would have to make peace with it. She had come to the end of an alleyway with no way out. This time though, it wasn't death stalking her, it was life.

"We serve an *intentional* God," Royce said adamantly. "He corrects mistakes; He doesn't make them. His ways are precise, and they are without error or fault. Do we always understand them? Of course not. But that wasn't His intention. Just look at the lives of Kim, Luciana, Rasheed, and Jarel. From my perspective as a child, I was simply loving people who needed to be loved. From God's perspective, however, I was an instrument that He would strategically use in each of their lives to fulfill a much higher purpose. He used *me* to produce the spark; He used *them* to produce the fire. You saw the present—death, emptiness, confinement. God saw the future—life, fulfillment, freedom. You saw one life that was destroyed. God saw millions of lives that would be created."

Words poured from Royce's mouth, a rhythmic flow of passion and intensity. "Your life is a series of choices. The time you wake up, the clothes you put on, the food you eat, the music you listen to, the shows you watch, the books you read, the job you maintain, the church you attend, the prayers you pray, the thoughts you dwell on, the words you speak, the people you invest in, the habits you form—thousands of decisions made every day that will ultimately shape your personality, your character, your hopes, and your dreams. Some choices will be made consciously while others will be made unconsciously. Some will appear miniscule while others will appear substantial. But they will all be equally significant. Those choices will form an intricate web that will be interwoven with the billions of choices made by everyone else who exists on the earth. Only an omnipotent and omnipresent God has the capacity to take every decision that has ever been made and every decision that will ever be made and knit them together to impact eternity for his glory."

New holograms manifested on top of the lake. Royce kept his eyes locked on Laurie as he spoke, although Laurie couldn't help but divert her eyes to watch what was happening in front of her. Scenes flashed from around the world displaying various cultures, ethnicities, and religions. Image after image surged into each other to produce a fluid motion picture: *children playing in mud puddles; workers rebuilding homes destroyed by tsunamis; women birthing babies; fathers kicking a soccer ball with their sons; friends laughing while playing cards; pastors preaching; teachers teaching; presidents saluting the flags of their nations; elderly couples walking in parks; babies taking their first steps; street performers dancing; monks sprinkling a blessing over visitors in their monasteries; mothers washing clothes by hand outside of their huts; boys skipping rocks across a pond; youth playing hockey on a frozen lake; tourists riding elephants into the jungle; church congregations worshiping; families celebrating with fireworks; rock climbers scaling cliffs; university students rallying; soldiers training; newlyweds dancing at their wedding; priests praying; bands performing on stage; artists painting on top of balconies; volunteers feeding the homeless; villagers cooking dinner over a small fire; surfers sitting on their surfboards watching the sunrise over the ocean; siblings feeling a baby kick in their mother's stomach;*

farmers harvesting their crops; couples stargazing; seasons changing; the universe expanding.

"Don't you see, Mother?" Royce marveled. "All of these lives are intertwined in some way. Their existence depends on the manner in which they all choose to pursue their most heroic life—their most abundant life. They need each other. They need *you*. You have no idea what eternal factors hang in the balance of your choice to not give up, to not give in, to not surrender to the pain. These people need you to live, and they need you to live *free*."

Chapter 18
Put to Death

Laurie moseyed aimlessly about, observing her surroundings—the barn on top of the hill, the willow's branches above her, the lake once again at rest. She stared at her reflection in the water, curious if her reflection was pondering the same things that she was tossing around in her own mind. Royce seemed content to give Laurie as much time as she needed to process the events she had experienced. He patiently waited by the willow's trunk, watching her pace back and forth.

"I have one last question," Laurie said, her voice interrupting the serene atmosphere.

"Of course, Mother," Royce said. It didn't seem to bother him at all that she still had questions. He offered her a courteous smile. "How can I help you?"

"Why did God allow you to die?" Laurie asked the question with the deepest sincerity. There was no anger or accusation in her tone. "You had already made an impact on your friends' lives, which was enough to set the butterfly effect into motion. So why? Why did God choose to take you?"

Royce acknowledged her question but did not respond immediately. Instead, he reached into his pocket and pulled out the ball of snow that he had sculpted in his palm. Laurie had completely forgotten that he had kept it. He knelt down and gently placed it back into the snow, burying it. Then, he stood to his feet, shook off his hands, and returned his attention to Laurie.

"You are right. I didn't need to die in order for their lives to be changed. But my death wasn't for them."

"Who was it for?" Laurie asked.

Royce's smile faltered, and his voice grew sympathetic. "It was for *you*, Mother."

"I refuse to believe that," Laurie said quickly. "I can't believe that. I won't . . . It's not . . . Why? Why would He do that?"

"You live in a fallen world," Royce said. "That day, those boys made a terrible choice. A choice driven by fear and anger and pride. Could God have prevented it? Of course, He could have, but that was not His purpose. In the church parking lot, you told Pastor Scoggins that my life didn't need to be saved. And you were right, it wasn't my life that needed saving. It was yours."

Laurie opened her mouth to protest, but her words were cut short. Someone, *something*, whispered to her. Like a gust of wind or an exhaled breath, it quickly passed through her, leaving unforeseen knowledge in its wake. The words that weren't words were there, where the soul and the spirit meet. From the depths of everything she had been and everything she would be, she knew . . . Royce was right.

Laurie's eyes fixed on the lake. She spoke in a daze, more to herself than to Royce. "God knew that the only way to redeem my life was to take yours."

"Yes," Royce said, following her gaze. "Often, there is more power in death than in life. God needed you to be at a place of total surrender. He saw the choices you were making and the direction your life was going. He knew that the only thing that would lead you to complete surrender would be complete brokenness. He could have chosen to save my life, but in doing so, you would have continued down the dark tunnel that you were traveling. It may seem harsh, but I hope that after all you have seen, you can at least begin to understand how He works. He never does anything out of selfish ambition or pride. It is always out of love."

"I understand," Laurie said quietly.

Royce knelt down in the spot where he had buried the small mound of snow and motioned to his mother. "I want to show you something."

Laurie stepped toward him. Royce began brushing aside snow, as if he was carefully excavating a fossil. Before long, a shape emerged. Little by little, the shape became more recognizable. When the snow was completely cleaned off of it, Royce picked it up. Laurie leaned in to take a closer look.

"It's a frog," Laurie said confused. "A dead frog."

Royce laughed, startling her. "Yes, it's a frog. But this is not an ordinary frog. This is an Alaskan Wood Frog, and it is absolutely remarkable."

"Why is it so remarkable?" Laurie asked. She had just experienced countless emotions that had left her physically, mentally and emotionally drained. She didn't understand why he suddenly wanted to talk about a frog. "Is this really . . ."

"Necessary?" he asked. "Not only necessary, but important." Royce held the frog at eye level, inspecting it with awe. "These frogs are an amazing specimen, Mother. They live in a climate that experiences freezing temperatures for several months out of the year. Most species could not survive in that environment, but the Alaskan Wood Frog has a unique way of coping."

"And what is that?" Laurie asked.

"Two-thirds of their body turns to ice, and they simply . . . freeze." Royce lifted the frog by the leg, and sure enough, it appeared to be frozen solid. "What is extraordinary, however, is that for days, and even weeks at a time, their heart stops beating and their blood stops flowing. From an organismal perspective, they essentially, die. But when the weather warms, their heart starts beating again, and their organs begin to function properly. They thaw, look for a mate, and begin storing food for the following winter. And when that time comes, they will have to repeat the same process all over again—life to death, death to life."

Laurie looked at the lifeless frog in the palm of Royce's hand. "I'm sorry, but I'm not exactly sure what I'm supposed to be seeing."

Royce eyed the frog with a look of admiration. "You see, Mother, in order for them to live, a part of them must die."

He turned the frog over in his hand. A thin layer of glossy ice highlighted the texture of its skin. Its face was outlined in black streaks while the rest of its body was coated in dull shades of brown and green. Small ice crystals lined the rims of both its eyes. The details of its features really were amazing. Royce smiled to himself as Laurie slowly reached up and stroked one finger down the frog's body.

"In order to awaken to Christ, we must die to ourselves," Royce said. "Therein lies the problem. Some people will say that you must live before you die; which is good from a motivational standpoint, but it misses the essence of what it means to pursue a higher standard of living. What people really need to learn is how to *die* before they *live*, especially when it comes to healing from pain. For example, in order to accept what is beyond your control, your desire to remain *in* control must be put to death. In order to forgive others, your bitterness must be put to death. In order to forgive yourself, your regret must be put to death. In order to apply your pain, your selfishness must be put to death. In order to believe in God's sovereignty, your pride must be put to death.

"Greed, lust, anger, resentment, fear, doubt, anxiety, shame, impatience, self-pity—whatever it is that is preventing you from seeing God more clearly must be put to death. Only then can you live in complete freedom. Oh, and Mother?" Laurie lifted her head and looked at Royce. "Just as the frog must continually repeat the process of freezing to death, you must continually repeat the process of dying to yourself. It cannot happen only once. It must happen repeatedly. Like we discussed before . . . one choice, one day at a time. And when you have weathered the storm and chosen to live in peace, you will find fulfillment. From death, comes life. God promises it."

The layer of ice around the frog began to dissolve. Water dripped through the cracks of Royce's fingers, as if an ice cube were melting in his hand. The colors of the frog grew more vibrant, and its skin loosened. Then, a heartbeat pulsed. Laurie tried not to blink, afraid that she might miss a millisecond of the phenomenon. As if waking up from a long hibernation, the frog was reborn from death to life. The frog stretched out its limbs, extending them to the tip of Royce's fingers. Royce walked to the edge of the water and knelt down. The frog raised its frail legs, and with a slight wobble, stepped off of Royce's hand onto the shore. Laurie felt like she was watching a child take his first steps. A small hop later and the frog was swimming away from them with tiny ripples flowing behind it.

Laurie always thought that getting the answers she wanted meant that she would finally be satisfied; as if the pain would suddenly disappear and she wouldn't be sad anymore and the world would finally make sense. But standing on the shore of the lake watching the way the ripples of water faded into each other, she realized that the point of her journey wasn't to live without the pain. It was to find peace *amidst* the pain. It was to find significance *within* the pain. It was to find freedom *despite* the pain. She had asked for answers, and she had received them. Now, the only thing left to do was to apply them. And that's what she would do. She would be intentional about pursuing her healing.

An object fell in Laurie's line of sight. It was so miniscule that the motion would have gone undetected if not for the calm and stationary presence of the world around her. She crinkled her nose and looked up. The object landed on her this time, hitting her directly between the eyes. It was light, weightless, cool.

Laurie held out her hand, and a snowflake floated into her open palm. It was tiny, yet each of its crystallized arms sparkled with distinct clarity. She held both of her hands together, catching three, four, five flakes. She tilted her hands back and forth and watched in fascination as the surface of the flakes reflected off of each other. *Like small mirrors*, she mused.

Royce removed his hat and started catching snowflakes on his tongue. For a mere second, he wasn't in a new body, and they weren't in a different world. Laurie was standing with her son in their backyard during the first snow of the year, and they were happy. There was no death or pain or sadness—only love. The memory spread warmth throughout her body.

The small flakes began falling harder as the atmosphere unleashed a rain shower of snow. Once again, she was seeing the world through a completely new lens. Snowflakes twinkled on the surface of the water like rays of sun setting across an ocean. The willow's branches absorbed layers of the tiny mirrors, making it appear as if the tree were wearing a shimmering wig. The barn on top of the hill was given a new roof, smooth and glassy and illuminant. Laurie had never seen anything so beautiful.

She turned to Royce.

His arms were outstretched, his eyes were closed, and his head was tilted to the sky. His smile said that he would be content to stay in that moment forever. A line from his journal flashed before Laurie: "Never miss an opportunity to let the rain wash you clean." Her boy had not changed. He still had the same faith, the same joy, the same passion. Only now, he was in a place where death could no longer harm him and life was no longer bound by time. He was finally at rest. He was at peace.

He was redeemed.

Laurie stretched out her arms until they were fully extended. She watched snow flurries speckle her skin and settle onto her dress. In another world, Royce had looked at Uncle Billy while Uncle Billy had looked at the sky. Now, she was looking at Royce while Royce was looking at the sky. There was no mourning in heaven, only rejoicing.

Grateful tears formed in her eyes, and a grin spread across her face. She began to laugh. It started out small, as just a chuckle, but then it grew. Soon, she was laughing long and hard and deep. Her laughter turned into sobs of relief, which then turned into sobs of *release*. As her tears shed years of pain, joy that had all but grown extinct from her life began rejuvenating her spirit. The emotion that had lain dormant for years had finally awoken. Beside her, Royce started laughing as well.

Side by side, mother and son, they looked to the sky with outstretched arms and let the snow wash them clean. Together they cried, together they laughed, and together they *healed*.

Chapter 19
Unfinished Work

Royce and Laurie walked hand in hand back up the snowy slope toward the barn.

For Laurie, there was no way to grasp the emotions of everything she had just relived. The word *surreal* kept floating into her mind, but even that word seemed trivial in comparison with the things she had experienced.

As she trudged lightly through the snow, she tried to think back to when it all started. Why couldn't she have faced the pain and dealt with it? Actually, she had dealt with it, but not in ways that would cure it. Whether consciously or unconsciously, she had always found ways to camouflage it, to outrun it, to mask it, while in reality, her pain was the one camouflaging *her*, outrunning *her*, masking *her*. She had allowed it to gain control and dig its roots deeper and deeper into the soil of her soul.

When she was a child, she had retreated to imaginary worlds: dolls, books, trees houses. She was simply too naive to fully understand the implications of how her childhood was being violently abused. During her teenage years, she had taken refuge in friendships (including her siblings) and busied herself with extracurricular activities after school. As she grew into adulthood, she had found her identity in her husband and further repressed the memories of her past. After Royce's death, she had found herself in the bottle, burying the pain and erasing it permanently from her memory—or so she thought. Her life had been a distraction from the reality that lay just beneath the surface of her most vulnerable self. The World of White had resurrected those issues and brought them into the light. It had revealed the very things she had tried desperately to keep hidden. But now, things had changed. Things would be different. *She* would be different.

The sting of the memories had not suddenly disappeared. It was still there, throbbing like a fresh bruise. The difference this time, however, was that she did not feel littered with defeat. She felt lifted by victory. She realized that she had lived with her demons for so long that she no longer knew what genuine freedom felt like. Even when she thought she was happy, it had only been a film covering her eyes that would soon wash away, revealing her true identity. The pattern had repeated itself over and over and over again.

Until now.

They slowed their pace as they approached the barn. Laurie turned to Royce. "This may seem like a silly question, but out of all the things you have shown me, what is the very first step. Where does the healing start?"

A warm smile touched Royce's lips, and he pointed to his head. "It starts here. *You* start here."

"In my mind?"

"In your mind," Royce affirmed. "Before this journey started, I told you that these were lessons designed specifically for your healing. Each one of them focuses on learning to control your mental state of mind. When things that happen that are beyond your control, it often involves learning how to forgive others. When things happen that are within your control, it often involves learning how to forgive yourself. In both instances, you will need to learn how to apply your pain and believe in the sovereignty of God. All of these areas— things beyond your control, forgiveness, application, and God's sovereignty—are areas in which you must first conquer mentally. This is often the most difficult step, but once it is achieved, it makes the physical process much easier."

"How so?" asked Laurie.

"There are many practical and professional methods that could be, and should be, utilized to help someone in their healing process—seeking wisdom and guidance through counseling, confiding in others for prayer, transitioning to a new profession or a new location, developing new relationships, finding a new church home, taking proper medication, reading books, journaling, attending conferences, investing in new projects. There are numerous outlets that can assist someone's venture to finding peace. God knows that not all people will be able to find freedom in their thoughts alone. And frankly, He didn't design human beings to function that way. While thoughts alone will not bring healing, it is true that—"

"It all begins in the mind," said Laurie.

"Yes," Royce beamed. "Thoughts birth mind-sets, mind-sets birth actions, actions birth habits, habits birth lifestyles, and lifestyles birth futures. Once you have decided what you will choose to believe and have bound yourself to those beliefs no matter what opposition you may face, then you will be able to pursue other measures with much more success. It will add significance to the journey."

As Royce finished speaking, he zipped up his jacket and fit his wool hat snuggly over his head. Then, he pulled his gloves from his pocket and squeezed them onto his hands. Once he had finished, he looked at Laurie and held out his arms. She folded into them, grateful for his embrace.

"Royce, I . . . it just . . . I'm not sure what to say." Laurie fumbled to find the right words but finally gave in. "Well, I just wanted to thank you."

"Of course, Mother. Although, I'm not the one you need to be thanking." He winked and pulled his parka hood up. "And speaking of *Him*, He allowed me to take you on this journey, but after it—"

"I have to go," finished Laurie.

Royce laughed. "That's right. You are getting good at thinking like me. It happens when you stay in this place long enough."

"Why can't I go with you?" Laurie asked directly. "Why do I have to go?"

"Because there is more, Mother. So much more! You have died to one life, and now, it's time that you awaken to another. You can't waste any more time. That life is waiting for you to begin."

Laurie looked at him with slight confusion. "But I don't know what life I'm in . . . whether I'm alive or—"

"He will show you," Royce said. "He always does."

"But where will I *go*?" she persisted, her voice panicking. "How will I function without you there? What happens if I can't figure out the answer? If I don't know what to do?"

Royce scanned the barren land, taking in its scent, its mystery, its wonder. "There is a voice that created every planet, in every solar system, in every galaxy, in the expanse of the universe. A voice that spoke life into billions of organisms that have billions of designs that serve billions of purposes. A voice that coddles the stars like infants and calls the sun to rise. A voice that commands death to breathe again. A voice that exists where reality ends and faith begins, where your past, present, and future collide." Royce leaned in closer, speaking softly. "That voice is alive, and it *knows your name.* How will you know what to do? Follow that voice, Mother. Allow it to guide you. That voice is God's love, and God's love never fails."

Laurie wrapped her arms around Royce one last time. There were no tears and no remorse. All she felt was gratitude. As she hugged him, she could feel herself being made whole, and she knew that she would have the strength to endure whatever journey lay ahead of her.

They finally parted and faced each other. For a moment, he was the same boy that Laurie had always known, standing awkwardly with dirt in his hair and a Spider-Man backpack on his shoulders. She smiled. "I love you, my sweet son," she said.

"I love *you*, my precious mother. I always have, and I always will."

Royce turned and walked in the direction from which he had arrived. His body bobbed back and forth as he passed the barn and descended down the hill that lay behind it. Laurie desperately wanted to call after him, but she knew that she couldn't. He had accomplished what he had been sent to accomplish. His job was done. Now, he was being called home as well.

Royce paused one last time to turn around and wave, his smile radiant and his features glowing. Then, he continued his journey.

Like the sun setting, his body slowly disappeared from view as he sank down the slope of the hill. Finally, he vanished completely.

Laurie heard a *sputter*. She wheeled around to find the white horse standing behind her. Its white coat shimmered as it had the first time she had seen it, perfect, without blemish. She knew that it was there to lead her out of The World of White.

She approached the horse, prepared to follow it. Instead, it lowered its head and elegantly bowed to its knees. Laurie didn't need to be instructed on what to do.

She walked to the horse's side and placed one hand on its neck. The feeling was euphoric. Like Royce, energy flowed throughout its body, igniting her fingertips and the palm of her hand. It was warm, producing electricity without electrocuting. The horse inhaled and exhaled, life expanding and contracting. She had never experienced such power contained within a living being. Laurie eased onto the horse's back. Immediately, it rose to its feet and embarked down the hill toward the lake.

The experience riding the horse was no different than it had been observing it. Laurie had watched the horse glide effortlessly through the snow on the way to the barn, its movements calculated and smooth. Each step lured her into a hypnotic trance.

And so was the journey back to where it had all started.

They strode past the lake and the willow, up the embankment of the hill beyond them. Each hoof sank into the snowy surface as if it were dough, soft and cushioned. The ground ran beneath them without running. The land passed around them without passing. Light shone down on them without shining. They were present, in each moment individually, unscathed by time or reality. Step after step, stride after stride.

Laurie blinked, and the horse came to a halt. They had already arrived. Before she could react, the horse knelt down, allowing her to slide easily off of its back onto the ground. Laurie stood and rotated in a circle, analyzing her surroundings with a new sense of awareness. The landscape, of course, was the same, but Laurie knew that she had changed. Like the white hills that stretched farther than she could see, she too felt like the black stains had been removed from the mountains of her heart.

As if it knew that Laurie had a long journey ahead of her, the horse turned and trotted back up the hill. Laurie watched it go, feeling that a piece of her soul was retreating. When it reached the summit of the hill, the horse turned and peered down at her, as if offering her one last farewell. It reared back on its hind legs and whinnied loudly. Then, it galloped out of sight, leaving Laurie alone once more.

She knew that the time had come to return. Her eyes swept across the land one last time. She soaked in every detail—the crisp feeling in the air, the way the ground fused into the sky, the lukewarm snow between her toes, the silk of her dress. It was all a part of her now, and it always would be. Laurie sat on the ground, stretched out her legs, and lay flat on her back. She stared at the sky and watched the sky stare back at her. Seconds later, she closed her eyes.

The silence that already existed was muted. Soon, she felt her surroundings fold in around her, as if the world's arms had swaddled her in a blanket. There was no pain, only a faint sense of evaporation. She didn't fight it. She allowed herself to drift away, like a raft cast out to sea. Slowly, she slipped from the world that had saved her back into the world that needed saving . . .

* * *

Laurie's eyes shot open.

Air surged into her lungs, sending her into a fit of coughs. She seized the sheets and desperately tried to calm her hyperventilated breathing. Her eyes darted back and forth across the room. Where was she? *When* was she? She tried to comprehend her current state, but the lack of oxygen made it difficult to concentrate. *Inhale and exhale*, she thought. *Slowly . . . again . . . and again . . . and again . . .* Laurie spoke to herself as if she were comforting a child. Gradually, the feeling of vertigo started to pass, and her labored breathing returned to normal.

She sat up in bed. Clothes still lay scattered on the floor, and an empty pill bottle still lay by her side. She still clutched the sheets in her hands, as if attempting to grasp her new reality. Her bed. Her apartment. She had definitely returned. Outside, the rain had stopped, but droplets of water still clung to the glass pane. How long had she been gone?

Laurie shut her eyes and tried to recall the miracle that had just happened. She wanted to savor every component—the universal depth of the horse's eyes, the flickering of the white bonfire flames, the way the holograms danced on the surface of the water without causing any ripples, *Royce's smile*. She didn't want to lose any of it. Images danced through her mind. They were only glimpses, highlights, snapshots, but their core was etched inside Laurie in a way that could never be erased. She wanted to remain in those moments forever, but she knew her return served a much greater purpose.

She finally willed her eyes open and looked around the room again. An open book lay on the ground next to her bedroom door. She swung her legs out of bed and walked over to it. Before she even knelt down, she recognized it. The tattered edges. The worn cover. The shimmering Celtic symbols. It was Royce's journal. She must have dropped it while stumbling across her bedroom.

As she picked up the book, a picture slipped out of its pages and fell to the floor. Laurie picked it up and held it close to her face. The picture showed Royce standing outside in the rain. His arms were outstretched, and he was laughing. She turned the photograph over, and written across the back in Royce's handwriting was a single quote:

> *"Life isn't about waiting for the storm to pass. It's about learning how to dance in the rain."*

Laurie slid the picture back inside the journal and held the book to her chest. She knew that the pain would never completely disappear, but that wasn't the point. She had been shown that freedom could be found within the shame, that joy could be found within the sorrow, and that victory could be found within the defeat. She immediately thought about the following day, how the sun would rise and how she would be forced to wake up to the rest of her life.

The journey to healing would be tedious, wearisome, and long. But she would endure. She was no longer a soul who turned back. She had been given a second chance. She had been reborn. And now, she knew exactly what had to be done.

Chapter 20
Hope

It was a day that artists would have wanted to paint. John Mark's mother was at the Roses retail store buying him a pumpkin to carve the following day with his friends. Ms. Sempsrott was sipping hot tea in her living room and finishing a scarecrow decoration to hang on her classroom door. "Cotton Top" Cody and his dad were jumping in a pile of colored leaves that they had raked earlier that afternoon. Mrs. Cloggins, from 4B, was baking pumpkin bread while still humming the song that her mother used to sing while tucking her in bed at night. The homeless man down the road was sitting by the green bench. He was still homeless, and the bench was still green, although it had been repainted, and he now ate at a small soup kitchen that had opened up the week before. Mr. Perkins was delivering the mail and wearing a real mask in the spirit of Halloween. "Nike Man" was running, "Sweet Tooth Nana" was eating, and "Ma'am Talk-A-Lot" was waving her hand weights wildly in the air. The town kept its rhythm and danced to the beat of the world, and everyone carried their day in their pocket. That's the only thing that people wanted to do on a day that was perfect; a day that artists would have wanted to paint.

But while people smiled and laughed and hummed the earth's melody, something of much greater significance was happening. If you drive past the old Morganton Baptist Church and curve around Bradburn's Grocery, the road eventually forks off onto Hideaway Street. At the end of Hideaway Street, past the long row of charcoal apartments and the new bait shop, a crooked "Dead End" sign leans against a rusted, iron gate. Beyond that gate, over the pothole-infested hill, a field with jagged rows of tombstones lies dormant— even *that* one. The one that no longer has a woman collapsed in front of it with the smell of "too much to drink" on her breath. In her place, you will find a letter leaning against the grave with the following words written on it:

My dear son,

I just wanted to thank you. I was so lost before, and in many ways, I still am. I know that healing takes time and that I still have a long way to travel on my road to recovery. But I also know that I am no longer greeted by the same great sadness each morning when I wake up. A new feeling has started to take its place. It is a feeling that my journey will not end in defeat. It is a feeling that the canvas of my life can be repainted. It is a feeling of redemption. It is a feeling of hope. It grows inside of me, slowly but steadily. And it is because of what you have shown me, not only through your life, but through your death.

You have shown me what it means to change, what it means to love, and what it means to change others by our love. You have shown me what it means to choose to see people through His eyes. You have shown me that we serve an intentional God, that our pain is never wasted, and that we are each born with a unique purpose in this universe.

You have shown me what it means to live and what it means to live free.

I understand that I will always have to live *with* my pain, but I can refuse to live *in* my pain. I see that now, more clearly than I ever have before. So, I will do my best to fight the good fight, to finish the race, and to keep the faith— and then, once God is done with me, I will see you again. Until then, know that I love you with each waking second.

Mom

Somewhere above the trees and beyond the graveyard of a small north Georgian town, there is a highway. On that highway, there is a small car driving west, toward the setting sun. A woman sits behind the wheel with orange and pink clouds reflecting off of her sunglasses. Her windows are down, her radio is on, and her hair whips freely in the wind. And she is smiling—a deep, *genuine*, smile.

Acknowledgments

To Dance was never intended to be a full-length novel. In the beginning, it was just "Colorblind"—a 14,000-word short story that explored the thoughts and emotions of a ten-year-old boy experiencing racial injustice. When my wife read the story, however, she flippantly made the comment, "I just want to know what happens to the boy's mother." I had never considered the idea, but when I did, a 61,000-word manuscript popped out. And so, I think it's only fitting to first thank my wife, Megan. Throughout this journey, she has kept me mentally and emotionally grounded, helped clarify my over analytical thinking, and patiently listened to my endless thought spirals. Ultimately, it was her curiosity that birthed a new world. I'll forever be grateful.

I was actually living in Indonesia with my parents when I started this book. They offered me a quiet environment to reflect, allowed me to disappear for hours at a time to write, and most importantly, introduced me to Indonesian white coffee. The combination of those three elements helped make this dream become a reality. I will never be able to thank them enough for their service and their sacrifice, both of which instilled in me a passion for local and global ministry.

Jenifer Pauls read and reread this manuscript. Her insights and sage advice (as well as her beautifully written sticky notes) helped smooth out the ragged edges of the book. Editing a friend's work can be intimidating, tedious, and time consuming, so I don't take the help for granted. (I guess I should also thank her husband, Brian, who sweat off ten pounds in our much-hotter-than-it-should-be home while Jen and I discussed everything literature. You are the real champion, B.)

A huge thank you goes to Christian Faith Publishing for being willing to take on this project. Throughout the course of publication, their staff was extremely professional and communicated thoroughly. It was truly a joy to work with them (particularly my publication specialist, Sarah, who graciously fielded all 9,456,445 of my questions). I hope this book blesses CFP as much as they have blessed me.

The final thanks goes to my Lord and Savior, Jesus Christ, who supported my goals and believed in my vision long before he knit me together in my mother's womb. He is the author of tomorrow and the hope of today. He is the reason we can dance in the puddles and sing to the sky when the clouds grow dark. Thank you for showing me how to live, and how to live free. It's all for you, Jesus.

Appendix

1. While the story "There is More" (August 29, 2016: Walks
    Home) is my own, the principles were inspired from a poem
    I read in John Maxwell's book, *Success, One Day at a Time*. I
    thought the lines were too powerful to be left dormant, so I
    created a narrative to help bring them to life. The original poem
    reads below:

    > Do more than exist; live.
    > Do more than touch; feel.
    > Do more than look; observe.
    > Do more than read; absorb.
    > Do more than hear; listen.
    > Do more than listen; understand.
    > Do more than think; reflect.
    > Do more than just talk; say something.
    > —Author Unknown

2. The chaos theory was popularized by an American mathe-
    matician and meteorologist named Edward Lorenz in the
    early 1960s. Its nickname, the butterfly effect, was coined after
    a paper he presented in 1972 entitled: "Predictability: Does the
    Flap of a Butterfly's Wings in Brazil Set Off a Tornado in Texas?"
    I was first introduced to the theory when I watched the movie,
    The Butterfly Effect (New Line Cinema, 2004), and it forever
    changed the way that I viewed making decisions. It is a powerful

concept and deserves to be explored. I encourage each of you to investigate it more in-depth!

3. The Alaskan Wood Frog is indeed a real frog, and it does indeed "freeze" during the winter months. How this happens involves a lot of science, and considering that I am not very scientific, I'll leave it to the experts to explain. Research this amphibian online for more information.

Discussion Guide

Part 1: Colorblind

August 18, 2016: What to Do When the Clouds Grow Dark

1. What did Uncle Billy mean when he said, "Never miss an opportunity to let the rain wash you clean"?
2. Royce says, "That's how Mother had looked at the clouds, and that's how Uncle Billy had looked at the clouds. Both were looking at the same sky but had seen different things." Do you tend to see situations like Mother or Uncle Billy? Explain.
3. Royce hints briefly at an earlier memory that might explain why Mother sees the world the ways she does. To what extent do our circumstances determine our outlook on life?
4. Unwrap Royce's comment: "The darker the clouds get, the harder it rains. But the way I see it, the harder it rains, the cleaner you get! You just have to learn to dance in the rain first."

August 29, 2016: Walks Home

1. When was the last time you made an effort to observe the details of the world around you? Recall that time, and share what you learned from that experience.
2. In the story that Royce records, the master teaches his student five principles about life: 1) We must do more than

think. We must reflect. 2) We must do more than look. We must observe. 3) We must do more than touch. We must feel. 4) We must do more than hear. We must listen. 5) We must do more than exist. We must live. Which of the five areas do you struggle with the most concerning the way you see the world? What is one practical step you can take in that area to choose to see things differently?

September 15, 2016: Masks

1. What "mask" do you most often catch yourself wearing and why?

September 22, 2016: Mother

1. Royce alludes to the fact that his mother has been "getting back on her feet" for two years. In the Bible, it says that there is a time for weeping and a time for laughing, a time for mourning and a time for dancing (Ecclesiastes 3:4). How do you determine when the time is right to make those transitions?

2. Are there any "bullies" in your life that refuse to allow you to stand up? Write a list of each one, describe the source of the pain, how long it has plagued you, and the manner in which it is preventing you from living your most heroic life.

October 10, 2016: The Field

1. Have you ever witnessed an injustice happening but you were too intimidated or afraid to do anything about it? What were your thoughts in that moment? Share about this experience.

October 10, 2016: Why We Run

1. Royce says, ". . . what we run *from* is much more important than what we run *to*." Do you agree or disagree with his statement? Explain.
2. Is there anything that you are trying to "outrun" in your life? What is the first step that you need to take in order to face it?

October 25, 2016: How to Pray

1. Royce comments, "Mother never prays anymore because she said that she has said too many prayers . . . Maybe Mother has run out of things to say, or maybe God sees the mess in the living room, or the smoky ashtray, or the brown bottle wrappings, and knows what she wants even without her asking." Analyze your prayer life. What, if any, factors have led to your prayer life growing stagnant?
2. What is one area that is preventing you from seeing people as God sees people? Like Royce, what is a simple prayer that you can pray to ask God to change your heart?

October 26, 2016: Things Change When You Pray

1. When was the last time that God answered a prayer but not exactly in the way that you had envisioned it? Share what you learned from that experience.
2. Have you ever prayed a prayer in which God's answer was "no"? What did that experience teach you about yourself, and what did that experience teach you about God?

November 3, 2016: Sadness

1. When speaking of his mother's sadness, Royce says, "Sometimes, it's not in her words, but in the rings under her eyes, or the shaking in her hands, or in her strewn lip-

stick, or in her messy hair. It comes in different forms but always with the same message." In what ways has your sadness presented itself before? How did you choose to handle the situation once it became apparent that you needed help?

November 8, 2016: A Boy Named Kim

1. In the last paragraph of the chapter, Royce says, "Some other kids saw the boys take off with my lunch, but they passed by on the other side of the hallway and didn't say a word. Maybe they were scared, or maybe they saw what I saw—that some people pick on other people because something is missing in their lives." Have you ever allowed the pain or dissatisfaction you are experiencing in your own life negatively influence those around you? Explain.

November 9, 2016: To Be Popular

1. Royce comments, "Isn't that what everyone really wants? To know that they belong? To know that they are important? To know that people like them?" Do you agree or disagree with this statement? How does people's search for meaning and acceptance influence their daily choices?
2. When was the last time that you did something to gain recognition at the expense of someone close to you? Share what you learned from that experience.

December 13, 2016: Choosing Teams

1. Have you ever had an opportunity to befriend an outsider or someone new to a particular social arena? Was the choice difficult or easy? Share about the feelings you had following the encounter and what the experience taught you about venturing beyond your comfort zone.

December 17, 2016: Tears

1. At the end of the chapter, Royce says that there "aren't any wasted tears." What memories bring tears to your eyes? Consider the different emotions that have made you cry. What do they say about you, your personality, and the things that burden your heart?

December 19, 2016: Finding Blue

1. Royce comments that maybe one day Ms. Sempsrott will find out that she has a "blue" too. What does he mean by this statement, and how can it be applied concerning the way we choose to see the world around us?
2. Have you found your "blue" yet? Explain.

January 8, 2017: The Boy with the Hat

1. When was the last time that you did something to help someone who was not of your same race, religion, or background? Share about this experience.
2. What excuses have you used, or perhaps been fed, that have prevented you from reaching out to those who are different than yourself?

March 7, 2017: A New Nickname

1. Have you ever had to sacrifice something in order for good to triumph? Explain that situation and what you learned from it.
2. Royce comments that his Uncle Billy used to always say, "Your pain isn't being wasted as long as it's helping other people." Do you agree or disagree with this statement? Explain how it might be applicable in your own life?

March 14, 2017: Scars Speak Louder than Words

1. In what way have your scars, physically or emotionally, communicated your life's story?
2. Which of your scars is the most significant? Share that story.

April 21, 2017: Sometimes We Just Know

1. Have you ever experienced a moment like Royce in which you felt like time was running out? How does our awareness of time directly influence our mind-set, our choices, and the attitude we possess each day?

Part 2: The World of White

Chapter 1: What Others Were Doing

1. In the midst of comfortability and convenience, we often don't think about people who are, at that very moment, experiencing circumstances less fortunate than our own. Further, we often don't even *think* to think about people who are experiencing these less fortunate circumstances. What is one step that you can take to bring awareness to these issues? Before you continue this study, take a moment to pause and pray for people who need God in a special way at this very moment.

Chapter 2: Remembered

1. Royce's tombstone reads, "He danced when the clouds were dark, sang when the storm was loud, and loved when others lost sight. This love will always be remembered." If you were to die tomorrow, what is the most dominant attribute that others would remember about you?

2. Draw two tombstones. On the first stone, write all of the qualities that you want to be remembered for when you die. On the second stone, write all of the qualities that you would be remembered for if you were to die right now. In an honest critique of yourself, compare and contrast the qualities you wish to be remembered for with the qualities you are currently demonstrating in your life. What is the first step you need to take in order to bridge the gap between the areas of inconsistency?

Chapter 3: Our Ghosts

1. The chapter begins with the quote, "We all have ghosts. Some loom larger than others, and some are disguised better than others, but they all exist. They linger deep within our thoughts, waiting to be called on stage to present their act in front of a deteriorating mind. And most of the time, they get applauded back on stage for an encore." Which ghosts from your past, consciously or subconsciously, have overrun the theatre of your mind?
2. Alluding to Laurie's ghosts, the text says, "They all rose within her, wearing different masks. Perhaps that was the hardest part of all—trying to decide which ghost, from which time, could cause the most harm." Which of your ghosts consistently cause you the most harm, whether physically, mentally, emotionally, or spiritually?
3. The text lists a number of different "masks" that Laurie's ghosts wear, all linked to particular senses of her body. Some are physical, and some are physiological. What masks do your ghosts wear daily that continuously remind you of their existence? Choose one your five senses and focus on how you can relinquish the control that that particular ghost has over you.

Chapter 4: The Pact between Demons and Men

1. Analyze the different "alcohols" that you use to cope with the demons in your life. What sensations/pleasures/peace do you gain from each of them?

Chapter 5: Bad Things and Broken Pieces

1. Why is that we tend to push away the people who love and care about us the most?
2. Are there any areas in your life that you have tried to be the judge over what is "good" and what is "bad"? How have each of these areas birthed a sense of entitlement in your mind?
3. Is there one person in particular who has attempted to support you and hold you accountable, yet you continuously push them away? What is one step that you can take today to mend that relationship and allow God to use that person in your life?

Chapter 6: God Has Alzheimer's

1. Laurie asks Pastor Scoggins, "Does God deliberately allow Satan to bring ruin on us?" In response, he says, ". . . it sounds like what you are really wondering is if God ever has an impure motive. And in that case, no, I don't believe his motives are flawed. God's only motive for us is love. Now, do I believe that sometimes God chooses to allow us to experience pain rather than removing it? Absolutely. But that too is driven by love. The Bible is full of stories where God used pain to fulfill his purpose." What is your opinion of Pastor Scoggins' response? Has there ever been a time in which you believe God intentionally allowed you to experience pain? Share what the experience taught you about yourself as well as what the experience taught you about God.

2. Has there ever been a time in your life where you feel like God has forgotten about you? Read and analyze the account of when John the Baptist sent messengers to Jesus while John himself was in prison (Matthew 11:1-15). In what ways does John's attitude reflect your own attitude concerning your current situation or a time in the past where you experienced pain? How does Jesus' response offer an explanation of how he views pain that we experience and the manner in which he chooses to comfort us?

3. Pastor Scoggins says, "God will do anything for his glory . . . even if that means orchestrating life through death." Do you agree or disagree with this statement? Explain.

4. Is there someone or something that you are "fighting" against rather than running to God with your concerns?

Chapter 7: The Battle

1. Has there ever been a time in your life where you prayed and "battled" it out with God? Share about this encounter.

2. Have you ever bluntly told God how you feel? Take some time to pray and share with God the specific things that are burdening your heart.

Chapter 8: What Had to Be Done

1. Have you ever attempted to take your own life? What were your thoughts and emotions in those final moments? How did they demonstrate your view about God, about the world, about your family, and about yourself?

Chapter 9: The World of White

1. In your opinion, who or what does the white horse represent?

2. Referencing the horse's eyes (in relation to Laurie), the text says, "The eyes searched the innermost parts of her

being—the heart of her soul. They knew her. She could feel it. They knew the person she was and the person she was not. They knew what she had done and what she had left undone. They knew her mistakes, her faults, her failures. And they didn't look away." What emotions does this passage evoke in you, and in what ways does it illustrate God's grace in our lives?

Chapter 10: Reunited

1. Shortly after Royce is reunited with Laurie, he tells her, "There is a difference between seeing and having vision, Mother. You have only seen what you have chosen to see within the parameters of your pain. The life He wants you to pursue is beyond the boundaries you have created for yourself." In what ways have you, consciously or subconsciously, allowed your pain to narrow your vision of the life God has called you to pursue?

2. Royce tells Laurie that everyone's journey to healing is unique and that there is no "fix all" solution—that her journey to healing will be her journey and hers alone. Have you ever caught yourself comparing your hardships, burdens, or pain to that of other people? Why do we feel the need to validate our own progress in those areas by comparing it to others?

3. Concerning Laurie's pain, Royce says, "To understand what to fix, we must find where you are hurt, and to find where you are hurt, we must locate the root of the suffering." Have you ever taken the time to pray, seek wisdom, and discover the root of your pain? If so, then share the journey that you took mentally and emotionally to unveil those hidden truths in your life. If you have never done that before, then choose one thing you will do to begin that journey this week.

Chapter 11: Amidst the Flames

1. Before Royce and Laurie embark on their journey together, Royce requests that she says a prayer. He concludes, "But not just any prayer. Pain will not heal itself, so in order for the healing to begin, you must make a conscious choice to seek new vision." Is there an attitude, mind-set, or focus that you need to change concerning the way you talk to God?

Chapter 12: A Picture Is Worth a Thousand Wounds

Lesson 1: "You must accept that some things are beyond your control."

1. When Laurie hears the first lesson, she is very disappointed because she claims to be aware of that fact. Royce responds, ". . . being aware of a particular knowledge and actually applying that knowledge are two different things. Knowledge without application is useless." What are areas in your life you have yet to accept, or have struggled to accept, that are beyond your control?
2. Royce points out that, "When things happen to other people, we feel no bitterness or anger toward God. But isn't it interesting that when things happen to us *personally*, we ignore the knowledge that we claim to accept?" Can you think of an experience that, when it happened to someone else, you were not bothered, but when it happened to you personally, you grew angry and offended at God?
3. Royce says that the void, ". . . is the space where people lose sight of *Him*. Where there should be love, there is hate. Where there should be joy, there is sorrow. Where there should be peace, there is unrest. Where there should be patience, there is haste. Where there should be humility, there is pride . . . When people do not make choices through Him, it creates a void of all that is whole and pure. Truth is removed." Royce goes on to say that Laurie was

birthed into the void that her father had created in his own life, which was a circumstance beyond her control. Is there any part of you that is bitter at the void you were born into? Are there any areas of your life in which the void that other people have created in their lives has negatively influenced your own? Have you ever assessed these emotions to differentiate what is within your control and what is beyond your control?

4. Concerning Laurie's father, Royce says, "If his choices were beyond your control, then the ability to fix those choices is beyond your control." Simply stated, what are areas that you need to relinquish control and surrender to God today?

Chapter 13: The Sound of the Door

Lesson 2: "You must forgive others and surrender your pain."

1. Royce states, "Often, what we find ridicules, He finds redemptive." Are there any people/issues in your life that you have never reconciled with because you might have found the situations ridiculous or insignificant?

2. Royce says to Laurie, "To say that your father does not deserve forgiveness is to imply that he deserves to be condemned. And to claim who is worthy of forgiveness and who is worthy of condemnation is to determine the fate of their soul . . . Is that there where you have landed yourself? Someone who possesses all wisdom and all knowledge and is qualified to determine whether or not someone lives or dies? Whether someone should be extended grace or sentenced to suffer for all eternity?" Have you ever fallen victim to this line of thinking—offering conditional forgiveness rather than unconditional love? Think of a situation in the past where feelings of entitlement hindered you from forgiving the way Jesus commands us to forgive. Share what you learned from that experience.

3. Royce comments, "You forgive, not for what it does *for* them, but for what it does *in* you." Think of a time when it was particularly difficult to forgive someone but you did it anyway. Share about the transformation that took place inside of you following the choice to forgive.

4. Within his explanation of what it means to "surrender your pain," Royce adds, "You see Mother, to say the right words is to forgive with your mouth, but to surrender your pain is to forgive with your heart." Are there any areas in your life where you have forgiven with your words but are still clinging to the bitterness that the pain has caused you? What is the first step you need to take in order to surrender those emotions to God?

Chapter 14: Water and Blood

Lesson 3: "You must forgive yourself and release your pain."

1. Laurie comments, "I think there is some truth to that though, that some people just need time. You don't think that time can heal wounds?" Royce responds, "*Intentional* time can heal wounds." Analyze how you choose to spend your time during seasons of healing. What routines or habits do you create? What relationships do you maintain or break? What does your prayer life look like? In what ways can you be more intentional in how you manage and focus the time you spend trying to heal?

2. Royce states, "The ability to forgive yourself is something you develop in spite of the pain, not in the absence of the pain." To develop this strength, he says that, "You must understand the power of winning daily battles, the evidence of unconditional grace in your life, and the significance of living in the present." Discuss your thoughts on each of these three components (referenced below), assessing the following: 1) How are they relevant in your own life? 2) Which is the easiest and which is the most difficult for you

to personally grasp? 3) What do they teach you about the nature and character of God? 4) What methods can you develop to apply them in your daily life?

A. Understanding the power of winning daily battles: "People misinterpret the effort it takes to forgive yourself. They view forgiveness, forgiving someone else as well as forgiving yourself, as a singular event. A onetime decision. A decision that, once made, makes the symptoms of pain, grief, guilt, and shame, all disappear. The assumption is that the eradication of the symptoms is directly linked to the decision to forgive. Sadly, that's not how it works . . . You must wake up each day and recommit to forgiving yourself. It is not a onetime fix. It is a daily fix."

B. Understand the evidence of unconditional grace in your life: "Forgiveness implies grace. When you forgive someone, you are showing a measure of grace to that person. Likewise, if you refuse to forgive yourself, then you are refusing to show grace to yourself. Essentially, you are condemning yourself . . . If you cannot accept that, then you are confiding more in your selfishness than in His *selflessness*. You would be claiming that your judgement is more powerful than His mercy. This is completely twisted. If He does not condemn us, then we have no right to condemn ourselves."

C. Understand the significance of living in the present: "Because of His grace, we have the opportunity to wake up each day and start over. Each sunrise offers us a chance to see the world differently, to change, to leave the past in the past. If you are too focused on the pain behind you, then you won't recognize His purpose in front of you. You can, and must, be fully invested in *this* day . . . in the pursuit of the abundant life that He has for you. You have enslaved yourself with chains in the past, but He has come to set you free in the present. Take hope in *today*."

3. Alluding to the concept of "releasing your pain," Royce says, "Too often, people cling to their pain as if they are trying to protect it; like it is one of their most sacred possessions. The notion of releasing something signifies that you are no longer holding it captive. You are allowing it to escape from confinement. When you choose to live in grace, you allow the pain to move, to be set free." What pain are you protecting in your life right now? What is the first step that you personally need to take to release that area to God?

Chapter 15: A Dozen Anniversaries

Lesson 4: "You must apply your pain."

1. Royce comments, "People always ask questions when they are in pain. That's natural, and there is nothing wrong with it. But, your healing rests in the motive behind the questions that you ask . . . Typical questions range from 'How is this fair?' to 'Why did I deserve this?' or even your question, 'How could He take everything from me?' They are all understandable and obviously driven by the emotion of the moment. However, the questions that should be asked are much more evaluative—'What are you trying to reveal to me through this experience?', 'How can I use this situation to impact other people?', and 'How can I apply these lessons to gain a better perspective on the abundant life you intended me to live?" Evaluate the questions that have consumed your thinking during times of heartache. Compare the questions that center around selfishness, pride, and frustration to those that center around humility, gratitude, and peace. In what ways can you adjust the motive behind the questions that you ask?

2. Royce alludes to the fact that, in her moments of greatest confusion and brokenness, Laurie only focused on what she had lost rather than what she still possessed—her own son. Have you ever experienced a situation where you allowed your pain to mask the blessings that you still possessed in your life? Share what you learned.

3. Royce states, "If someone has experienced something you have experienced, and they have found peace within it, you would be much more apt to listen to how they came to find that peace over someone who had no way of sympathizing with you but was trying to tell you how to overcome a situation." Think of a painful event you experienced in your life that could be uniquely used to mentor other people in a similar situation. Share about this experience and how you plan to apply this pain to impact others' lives in the future.

Chapter 16-17: The Last Cigarette and A Butterfly's Wings

Lesson 5: "You must believe in the sovereignty of God."

1. To what degree do you personally believe our choices influence the futures of other people? Evaluate and explain.

2. Royce explains the butterfly effect by adding, ". . . every decision you make, no matter how small or seemingly insignificant, can create a chain of events that influences mankind in a way that is beyond all levels of comprehension. Every choice you make and every choice you choose *not* to make has consequences. Those can be positive or negative. No detail of life is insignificant." Can you think of an example from your own life where a choice you made, whether positive or negative, led to a series of events that greatly impacted others? Can you think of an example from your own life where the choice of another person, whether positive or negative, led to a series of events that greatly impacted yourself? Share what you learned about the power of choice from each of these experiences.

3. Royce concludes, "Your life is a series of choices . . . thousands of decisions made every day that will ultimately shape your personality, your character, your hopes, and your dreams. Some choices will be made consciously while others will be made unconsciously. Some will appear miniscule while others will appear substantial. But they will all be equally significant. Those choices will form an intricate web that will be interwoven with the billions of choices made by everyone else who exists on the earth. Only an omnipotent and omnipresent God has the capacity to take every decision that has ever been made and every decision that will ever be made and knit them together to impact eternity for his glory." Why do you think this concept is so difficult for people to grasp, especially those who have experienced heartache and tragedy? Does the idea that God is sovereign over the entire universe bring peace to you personally? Why or why not?

4. Evaluate the different arenas of your daily life which require you to make decisions. In which arena do you make the most decisions? In which arena are those decisions the most impactful? What is one change you can make in your routine of choices that will have a greater positive impact on those you come into contact with every day?

Chapter 18: Put to Death

1. Have you ever experienced a tragedy or loss that you believe God allowed you to experience in order to return your focus to him? Share about this experience.

2. Royce elaborates, "In order to awaken to Christ, we must die to ourselves. Therein lies the problem. Some people will say that you must live before you die . . . What people really need to learn is how to *die* before they *live*, especially when it comes to healing from pain. For example, in order to accept what is beyond your control, your desire to remain *in* control must be put to death. In order to forgive

others, your bitterness must be put to death. In order to forgive yourself, your regret must be put to death. In order to apply your pain, your selfishness must be put to death. In order to believe in God's sovereignty, your pride must be put to death . . . Greed, lust, anger, resentment, fear, doubt, anxiety, shame, impatience, self-pity—whatever it is that is preventing you from seeing God more clearly must be put to death." What are areas in your life, whether physical, mental, or emotional, that need to be "put to death" in order for you to begin the healing process? What is the first step that you will take to accomplish this?

Chapter 19: Unfinished Work

1. Alluding to the power of your thoughts, Royce says, "Thoughts birth mind-sets, mind-sets birth actions, actions birth habits, habits birth lifestyles, and lifestyles birth futures." Analyze the thoughts that you allow to dominate your mind on a daily basis. Which ones breathe life, and which ones breathe death? What is one practical step you can take today to redirect your thoughts and change the way you think?

2. When Royce prepares to leave, Laurie worries that she will not know what to do. Royce responds, "There is a voice that created every planet, in every solar system, in every galaxy, in the expanse of the universe. A voice that spoke life into billions of organisms that have billions of designs that serve billions of purposes. A voice that coddles the stars like infants and calls the sun to rise. A voice that commands death to breathe again. A voice that exists where reality ends and faith begins, where your past, present and future collide. That voice is alive, and it *knows your name* . . . That voice is God's love, and God's love never fails." Have you ever been afraid to move on from your pain because you are unsure of how to live a normal life? Maybe living in complete freedom intimidates you because there is no lon-

ger a safety blanket of damaged emotions? What hope do Royce's words offer to you personally concerning the courage you need to face tomorrow?

3. The chapter ends with the quote, "Life isn't about waiting for the storm to pass. It's about learning how to dance in the rain." How does this quote reflect Royce's and Laurie's individual journeys throughout the novel? How can it be applied to your personal journey to healing?

Chapter 20: Hope

1. Is there someone who you need to write a letter to today? Maybe a family member, a co-worker, a friend, or even yourself? Perhaps, you don't need to write a letter to someone but to *something*—a memory, a regret, a fear, or an emotion. Consider the greatest areas in which you need healing. Write an email, note, or letter to that person/thing to begin the road to redemption.

Summary:

1. How does the metaphor of "dancing" manifest itself throughout the novel?

2. Which of the five lessons has been the easiest for you to implement, and which of the five lessons has been the most difficult for you to master?

3. What is the most significant lesson, principle, or truth that you learned from reading this book? How will you apply that to your life to bring healing to yourself and to others in times of pain?

4. Say a prayer to thank God for his mercy, his love, and the hope that we have in his sovereignty today.

About the Author

S tephen McClellan has been a middle school educator for the past six years. His passion for travel and global ministry has taken him to eleven countries on four continents to mentor youth on living life with purpose and intentionality. Stephen and his wife, Megan, live in Cleveland, Tennessee.

CPSIA information can be obtained
at www.ICGtesting.com
Printed in the USA
LVHW041743311022
732004LV00003B/383

9 781642 992311